Operation Auger

ERYL JONES

CANDY JAR BOOKS · CARDIFF
2024

To the real John Francis Metcalfe (Private), who won the Distinguished Service Medal in France, September 28th, 1918

The right of Eryl Jones to be identified as the Author of the Work has been asserted by him in accordance with the Copyright, Designs and Patents Act 1988.

Editor: Shaun Russell
Editorial: Will Rees & Keren Williams

ISBN: 978-1-917022-15-6

Printed and bound in the UK by
4edge, 22 Eldon Way, Hockley, Essex, SS5 4AD

Published by
Candy Jar Books
Mackintosh House
136 Newport Road, Cardiff, CF24 1DJ
www.candyjarbooks.co.uk

– PROLOGUE –

August 1944, Normandy, Northern France.

I t had been eight weeks since the Allies landed on the Normandy beaches and steady, but relentless, progress had been made into the heart of France. Numerous logistical problems caused momentum to be lost and the advance had decelerated into a stalemate. The failure to capture a large port on the Atlantic coast meant that supplies were still being unloaded at the temporary Mulberry harbours. Men and material were coming ashore at a rate well below what was needed and supply lines were getting longer daily.

The absence of reinforcements was causing the greatest concern to Allied commanders. Parachuting in airborne troops had been suspended because of unsustainable losses. Numerous artillery battalions, operating deadly 88 mm Howitzers, had encircled the occupied area and were blasting the cumbersome Dakota transport planes out of the sky at will.

The appearance in the Channel of the sinister type 22 U-boat was giving the brass another headache. Allied intelligence was well aware of the state-of-the-art submarine's existence. They knew it had the speed to outrun pursuing destroyers, and its revolutionary shape made it much harder to detect by sonar. However, they dismissed the threat as irrelevant because the latest received wisdom stated that only two had been completed and were not yet in service, and that it would be 1945 before any further type 22s would be ready. For once in the conflict, Allied intelligence was found to be wanting. At the end of July, the German Kriegsmarine had twelve type 22s in the submarine pens at St Nazaire, fully equipped and ready for action. The wolfpack prowled the Channel, hunting down the sluggish troop carriers and supply vessels with ease. Again, losses were unsustainable.

The inability to make further inroads into France meant that the Reich were able to further develop their vengeance weapons almost unhindered, but what gave the Allied commanders nightmares was that German scientists could win the race to the atomic bomb. The deadlock had to be broken. Could the answer to the impasse lie with two maverick Cambridge graduates – one the son of a textile baron, the other a lord of the realm?

– CHAPTER ONE –

57 BC, North Western France.

Lucius Paulus was not a soldier. He had no military training, held no rank, and yet for the last five years he had lived as one. Lucius was an architectural engineer with a massive chip on his shoulder. The elders of Rome had been quick to spot his flair and artistry. At the age of twenty-two, his full-time job was designing the expansion of the city. Lucius' forte was making the practical look beautiful. Every road, aqueduct and bridge he designed was brilliantly fit for purpose, displaying an elegance and splendour that was instantly recognisable. Lucius was paid handsomely for his talents and was feted all over Rome.

But that had been five long years ago. He had been summoned at the behest of Julius Caesar to follow in the wake of his all-conquering army, and design and oversee the building of haughty monoliths, paying homage to Roman extravagance. But eating soldier's rations and living in spartan lodgings was a million miles from what Lucius was used to, and his outrage at the lifestyle being forced upon him grew more intense daily. The anger was further fuelled by the fact that he had to ride three days in baking heat because Caesar had sent for him. His resentment of military authority burned in his soul like a furnace.

Germania and Gaul were now firmly under the rule of Rome's fearsome legions and Caesar stood at the English Channel, greedily eyeing Britannia as his next conquest. His generals urged caution. Transporting a vast army across even a narrow stretch of sea was a logistical nightmare. Moreover, they had no clue as to the strength and competence of the foe they would face. But Caesar had other ideas. The rich reserves of tin, copper and lead, and vast forests of massive oaks for shipbuilding were too rich a bounty for him to ignore. A messenger was dispatched to bring Lucius to Caesar's Channel headquarters.

Lucius was not impressed by Caesar's rank, bearing or leadership. He was even less so when he explained to Lucius why he'd been sent for.

'Lucius, I intend to invade Britannia, but my generals tell me that a seaborne invasion presents enormous difficulties. Not least of which, all our conquests thus far have been across land. We have no ships to hand and would have to muster the main fleet from the Mediterranean. It would take many years to build the vessels we need for such an undertaking and it would also require a huge, highly skilled workforce. Therefore, I want you to look into the feasibility of digging a tunnel under the sea from here to Britannia. I realise the enormity of the task but we have any amount of labour, and for the task at hand, most of it does not need to be skilled. I think it can be done.'

Lucius would have laughed out loud if he didn't

know the dire fate that would befall him for doing such a thing. He decided the best course was to humour Rome's most powerful man.

'Certainly, my liege,' Lucius agreed affably. 'When would Caesar require the report of my initial findings?'

'Seven days from today.'

Lucius just about managed to stifle a howl of derision. He knew the task was impossible, but his inner anger had now turned to a sort of morbid acceptance of his fate. He would play along with this insanity – in fact, he would embellish the joke to the nth degree and damn the consequences.

– CHAPTER TWO –

August 1939, North Western France.

Jack Covington never used his inherited title. In fact, he took great delight in not doing so. But when his parents died in a boating accident, he had no compunction whatsoever in accepting the title, along with a three thousand acre Oxfordshire estate, plus numerous investments and holdings. Not that he wanted to become a member of the landed gentry, but the newfound wealth which landed in his lap at age twenty-two would certainly fund his passion for many years to come.

To say he had been a massive disappointment to his father was an understatement. Lord Covington had been a career soldier and followed in his father's and grandfather's footsteps to Sandhurst and the Oxfordshire regiment, and like his antecedents, he'd retired with the rank of brigadier. What is more, he fully expected his son John to do likewise. However, things had not gone to plan. To begin with, Lord Covington had not planned on Lady Covington's inability to bear him a son and wouldn't countenance the possibility that it may have been his fault.

Years passed, and no heir was forthcoming. The

acceptance was that Lord Covington's younger brother James would inherit the title, and all that went with it, and should he pre-decease his elder brother, it would all pass to his eldest son, Charles. Then out of the blue, aged forty-five, Lady Covington found herself expecting a child, making her husband a father at fifty-two.

John, the heir apparent, was packed off to Eton and a place booked for him at Sandhurst – an appointment young John had no intention of keeping.

From an early age, John derived much humour from gently kicking against the traces. Much to the irritation (and non-compliance) of the family, he insisted on being called Jack. He was an outstanding pupil at Eton and was offered a place at Trinity College, Cambridge, to read the Classics and Archaeology, the latter of which was his passion and he graduated *magna cum laudae*. Jack looked forward to studying the Roman conquest of Europe, and was looking for backers to sponsor his research when news reached him of his parents' demise. His parents had virtually disowned him when he had chosen Cambridge over Sandhurst. Indeed, his father had unsuccessfully looked into the possibility of denying Jack the title of Lord Covington. The sudden death of the incumbent Lord made everything straightforward in terms of the inheritance. Estate solicitors had begun work on the complicated process of leaving everything to any future grandchild, rather than the wayward son. Lord Covington may not have been able to deny Jack the title, but he could certainly make sure he would not inherit anything else. Unfortunately, the boating accident happened before anything was signed, so everything passed seamlessly to Jack.

Ten years on, Covington was regarded as a world

authority on the Roman occupation of Western Europe. He was sitting on a log in a small copse, just outside of Calais, wondering if his latest project was too bizarre, even for him. Just in case, he had decided to conduct this investigation solo. The circumstances that had brought him to France were a mixture of luck, intuition and a photographic memory. During his many candle-burning hours of research in the bowels of Trinity College Roman archives, he'd come across a map, circa 60 BC. It was of a huge forest, many thousands of acres, near to what is now the port of Calais. He had promised himself that when time and finances allowed, he would investigate further, and not because it was a map of a huge forest – huge forests covered most of Europe in 60 BC. The map was incomplete. It had been torn deliberately along two sides, meaning three-quarters of the map was missing.

Covington had obtained special dispensation to bring the map with him – Trinity was not about to deny such a request from one of its most celebrated sons – and after a cursory recce of the site, he was going to head for the museum in Paris. Covington arose, picked up his borrowed bicycle and headed for Calais railway station.

The museum in Paris was a treasure trove of artefacts and documents, all meticulously catalogued and scrupulously maintained. Covington had solicited the help of a senior curator at the museum who had directed Covington to the section that was likely to bear fruit. There was a mountain of written records covering the Calais area, not unexpected as it was the hub from which the invasion of Britain had been launched. It would have taken Covington an inordinate amount of time to work his way through them all, and it was time he couldn't spare. Covington showed his section of the map to Didier Pascal, the museum curator, who looked quizzically at the piece of parchment.

'Something wrong?' asked Covington.

Pascal shook his head.

'It's just that this parchment is fairly rare. It's thicker than normal and was made for outside use, usually for things like building plans.'

Pascal's eyes brightened and he clicked his fingers.

'I've come across this forest before. There's a mystery about it,' he said, beaming. 'It covered an area over two hundred square kilometres, and most of it was felled by the Romans over three years in around 58 BC.'

'So what's the mystery, Didier?'

'No one knows what they did with the timber, but whatever it was, it must have been large scale to require that amount of wood.'

'Are there any more documents like this from that time?'

'Very few, but I know where they would be.'

Covington delicately examined each parchment. They were mostly designs for minor bridges or small military buildings, but nothing that looked as if it had a piece missing. He carefully rolled up the parchments and gently pushed them back into the stiff leather tube, where they'd been contained for nearly two thousand years. As he did so, a corner of parchment appeared at the other end of the tube. He removed the already examined parchments, and armed with a torch and pair of tweezers, he carefully began to tease the corner out of the tube. It came out with surprising ease.

'*Mon dieu!*' Pascal exclaimed. 'Human's have not laid eyes on that for two millennia.'

Covington slowly unfolded the parchment. It was a

9

map with one-quarter missing. Not daring to hope, Covington placed his map into the missing space – it fitted perfectly. It was a map of the Calais area, the English Channel and the south east of England. There was also a diagram of a bridge joining Calais and Kent.

Didier shook his head. 'I don't understand, surely the Romans weren't thinking of building a bridge across the Channel? Look, there is an inscription at the bottom.'

Covington took out his magnifying glass.

'What does it say?' asked Pascal.

'It says "Lucius Paulus" – and that is not a plan for a bridge, it's a plan for a tunnel.'

Covington and Pascal sat in a bistro a ten-minute walk from the museum, a late August drizzle having sent them indoors from their preferred street table.

'Shall I ask the question or will you?' asked Pascal.

'Be my guest,' replied Covington, leaning back in his chair.

'OK, what was Rome's most famous civil engineer doing this far west?

'Well, as you know, my dear Didier, structurally, precious little remains of over a thousand years of Roman rule – even in Rome itself. Thankfully for the likes of you and I, a lot of documentation does survive, and I have seen the name Lucius Paulus crop up from time to time in association with structures all over Europe. But there are two bigger questions. A man as intelligent as Lucius Paulus would have known a tunnel beneath the Channel was an impossibility, so why draw up plans for one? And how come one quarter of the map ended up in Cambridge and the rest in Paris, after being deliberately separated?'

A thoughtful silence ensued between the two.

'Perhaps Lucius was under orders to draw up the plans,' ventured Pascal.

Covington nodded. 'Caesar was certainly well-known for his fanciful ideas and, as the missing piece was of the forest, perhaps Lucius wanted to cover up the fact that it had been felled for no good reason other than chasing a white elephant.'

'Did Lucius Paulus ever go to Britain?' asked Pascal.

Covington shook his head. 'No evidence that he did, but of course that doesn't mean he didn't. He seemed to disappear after about 52 BC. Probably died – very few Romans lived passed the age of forty-five. He must have fallen from grace somewhat though, because a man who'd made such a contribution to Roman architecture would have been entitled to an elaborate funeral, which, of course, would have been comprehensively written about. There should have been busts of him all over Rome.'

'Still doesn't answer how the missing map piece got to Cambridge, does it?'

'No,' agreed Covington. 'Nor does it answer why.'

The café owner switched on a large wireless that occupied a significant part of the counter. After a few seconds, it wearily crackled into life and the patrons stopped their chatter to listen to the news.

'Not good?' Covington enquired.

'Not good,' Pascal concurred. 'The German army is massing on the Polish border, up to five divisions. You'd better think about getting back to England.'

'Not before I've had one last look around the area in question.'

'In that case,' Pascal advised. 'Look up a guy called Juste Gilbert. He's a caretaker at the Mairie de Calais and a bit of a local expert on the Romans – what you would

11

call an enthusiastic amateur perhaps?'

'I'll do that,' said Covington with a nod, 'but I'll just mention the disappearing forest rather than the map for the time being. Probably best if we both keep shtum about that and the phantom tunnel for the time being, or they'll be carting us both off to the local sanatorium for bewildered historians. OK, if I hang on to the map for a while? I'll post it back to you from Calais.'

'Of course, and *bon chance mon brave.*'

Covington tracked down Juste Gilbert and found him eccentric but charming and only too pleased to impart his knowledge, even if his English was slightly suspect.

'The forest, it disappeared in three years,' explained Gilbert in his Sunday best English. 'I think it was for mine, to stop the roof falling down.'

'But there are no deposits around here to be mined. No ore of any kind or coal, so what were they mining? Besides which, what happened to all the spoil?'

'Spoil?' queried Gilbert. 'What is spoil?'

'All the stuff they brought out of the ground,' Covington explained.

'Ah, follow me,' said Gilbert. He strode off in the direction of the beach.

While still a good mile and a half from the shore, Gilbert came to a halt just where the ground started to gently rise.

'We now stand on what you call spoil. Before Roman come, sea would come up to here. Soil very different here than over there,' said Gilbert, pointing in the direction from whence they had come. 'Photo from aeroplane make it easy to see in summer when it gets very dry.'

'How much is there of it?' Covington asked.

'About two kilometre that way.' Gilbert indicated, pointing to the sea. 'And three kilometre that way, and that way.' He pointed to both his left and right.

'And how deep?' Covington pointed to his feet.

'Where we stand now used to be high above sea, like Dover.'

'A cliff you mean?'

'Yes, cliff, about fifty metres high.'

'Now, that is a hole that would take some filling,' Covington mused out loud.

'Come,' said Gilbert, 'I must show you the road that vanishes, just over there.'

The pair stood on a nondescript country lane, its straightness the only thing vaguely Roman about it.

Again Gilbert extended his arm. 'That way to old town, now gone, and that way it stops, the road to nowhere.' Gilbert pointed in the opposite direction.

The road, in fact, came to an abrupt halt at the foot of a small horseshoe-shaped hill. Covington checked his bearings and felt a slight tinge of disappointment when he realised the road ran parallel to the sea, not heading out under it.

Covington was booked on the early morning boat train, and after making as many map references as he was able before dusk fell, he retired to his hotel for an early night. The slow boat trip across the Channel would give him time to reflect on his latest findings. As it turned out, his mind would be preoccupied with matters a world away from Roman history.

At dawn that morning, German troops crossed the border into Poland. Covington thought it prudent to hang onto the map.

– CHAPTER THREE –

Three weeks later, Oxfordshire, England.

The three weeks since war had been declared passed like a blur to Charles Covington. True to family tradition, he became a soldier but even his meteoric rise through the ranks was above expectations. He had breezed through Sandhurst, heading the class in just about every department, and now held the rank of Major at just twenty-six. But unlike the rest of the Covingtons, he held no malice against his cousin Jack, the family's black sheep. Indeed, they had become firm friends. He had three days' embarkation leave before joining the BEF to be shipped to France. Jack had insisted that he join him for lunch before he went, but Charles suspected that it was something more than a farewell meal together.

Jack was there to greet Charles at the front door and the welcome was both warm and genuine. After lunch, they sat out on the patio, sipping Napoleon brandy. Jack unexpectedly leaned forward and blurted, 'Charles, I want to do something.'

Now realising his suspicion was correct, Charles said,

'By something, I assume you mean to help dear old Blighty defeat the nasty hun. Well, let's face it, Jack, a soldier's life is not for you, and you're too old anyway. But I'm sure your extraordinary talents could be put to better use in the service of your country. The question is, what?'

'Well, the whole of the estate is now let out to tenant farmers who I'm sure are doing their bit as food producers. Besides which,' Jack reasoned, 'what use am I here? I don't know a Brussels sprout from a bull's balls.'

'Remind me not to come here for Christmas dinner,' said Charles, 'but I do have an idea. You have spent your life looking for things, clues if you like, from examining terrain. One of the recent new tools in your box has been aerial photography. Photo reconnaissance is going to be a major weapon in this war, and it is going to need an army of specialist people to examine all these photos and spot things that are out of place. New, weren't there yesterday, that sort of thing. Besides which, you've travelled extensively in Europe. You'd be perfect.'

'And with the added bonus of being really interesting!' Jack enthused, 'When do I start?'

'Well, you haven't heard this from me,' said Charles, 'but the photo rec boys are based at RAF Medmenham. I'll call in there and see the station commander on the way home and tell him to expect a visit from you.'

'That's six miles down the road!' exclaimed Jack. 'I could live at home!'

– CHAPTER FOUR –

September 1943, RAF Medmenham, Buckinghamshire, England.

As expected, Covington took to working for the Central Interpretation Unit like a duck to water. The strings Charles had pulled were obviously the right ones, as Covington was in uniform and had begun training within a fortnight of Charles' visit. He was now an elite interpreter and a member of the select team that included the famous Constance 'Babs' Babington Smith, she of Peenemunde fame. Covington had struck up a friendship with Frank Ledbetter, another outstanding Cambridge student who'd studied Geology and Geography and had joined CIU straight after graduating in 1939.

Covington had found him a soulmate; they had so much in common. They shared the same off-beat sense of humour and both had an unquenchable passion for their chosen subject. Both had also gone against their parents' wishes but for very differing reasons. Ledbetter had two older sisters, who were a disappointment to his father, for no other reason than being the wrong sex. Ledbetter's father desperately wanted a son to join him in his cloth manufacturing business, and he could not conceal his joy when Frank was born. However, joy soon turned to anger and then bitterness when the boy had contracted polio at age six. He was ten before he could walk unaided and was destined to use a stick for the rest of his life. His father, though he never said it out loud, didn't want a cripple as a partner, thinking it would reflect badly on the company, and had very little to do with Frank's upbringing. In fact, he treated Frank as if he was mentally sub-normal. Frank was anything but. He overcame all sorts of prejudices throughout his young life to become the top student in his year at Cambridge – all driven by a steely determination to prove his father wrong.

The pair, along with their colleagues, made a great team, each one bringing something different to the table. A young WAAF came into their office one Monday morning and handed a note to Babs. She read it and then asked for everyone's attention.

'We've been summoned to a meeting in Hut C at ten this morning. All of this unit must attend.'

Speculative chatter filled the air as the team gathered in Hut C just before ten o'clock. Air Vice-Marshall Haverthwaite entered and everyone rose to attention.

'OK, everyone relax,' said Haverthwaite, 'but please pay close attention. What I have to say is very important. Everyone knows that this war will not end until Germany has been driven out of all the occupied countries and that, of course, will necessitate a landing by Allied Forces on mainland Europe. I don't think I'm giving away any great secrets in that statement.'

Polite laughter ensued. Rumours about D-Day had been rife for months.

'We still don't know when and where, or at least that's what the brass are telling us,' Haverthwaite continued, 'but plans are now being formulated, and that's where you come in. Most of the reconnaissance planes here at Medmenham are being taken off normal duties, and for the foreseeable future will be photographing every inch of the French Atlantic coastline from Dunkirk in the north to Bayonne in the south. You too will be taken off your present duties and will be full-time studying these prints, until we have the most comprehensive picture of France's Atlantic coastline. We want to know where every sand dune is, every high and low water mark, how deep the water is in every bay, and probably most importantly, the whereabouts of German troop concentrations and defence batteries. If a Frenchman throws a ball for his dog on one of these beaches, I want to know about it. As each film comes in, you will be told what to look for specifically, and as each of you has a speciality, the photos will be distributed accordingly. We expect the first planes to return by fifteen hundred hours tomorrow, so make sure you clear your stations by then. Good luck everyone, that is all.'

– CHAPTER FIVE –

December 1943, RAF Medmenham, Buckinghamshire, England.

'Jack, will you take a look at this? Frank says there's something odd about it. We're wondering if Fritz is up to something. You were in Calais in '39, weren't you? See if you can spot the oddity.'

Babs and Ledbetter approached Covington's table, brandishing a couple of photographs each. Covington lay back in his chair with his hands behind his head. 'If D-Day is going through Calais, I think it only fair to warn you that it's just possible the Germans might already be using the dock facilities.'

'We're aware of that, you silly Lord of the realm, but young Frank here has a bee in his bonnet about a geographical anomaly.'

Covington shook his head. 'It's just not right. It could be something sinister that's been camouflaged. Whatever it is, my gut feeling tells me it's not right geographically.'

'Let's have it under the magnifier then and we'll have a look.'

As soon as Covington saw it he was transfixed. Ledbetter was wittering in his ear. 'Look here, Jack, there are cliffs to the west and east, and the Channel to the north, and coastal grassland to the south. It's an area of roughly seven square miles and it looks as if the vegetation has just burnt off in the summer heat. It just doesn't make any sense.'

Covington continued to stare at the photo. There it was, just as Pascal had said – the spoil heap, standing out like a neon light in a monastery.

'Jack, Jack, are you still with us?'

'Sorry, both, just got carried away. I do know what it is but I would like to check something with some photos I have at home first. I'll bring them in tomorrow. But rest assured, it has nothing to do with German skulduggery. Before you knock off, Frank, could you check to see if you have a pic of the area just slightly to the southwest of this one?'

'Should be one in this bundle – here we are.' Ledbetter handed Covington the photo.

Covington's hands trembled as he placed it under the magnifier. There was no mistaking it. There it was, narrow and gun-barrel straight. The road to nowhere.

Covington returned to Medmenham the next day with one-quarter of a two-thousand-year-old map in his briefcase. When he got to his desk he laid out the parchment next to the two photos from the day before. Ledbetter and Babs were already in, and heading his way as he laid them side by side.

'So then, is his Lordship going to enlighten us after yesterday's cloak-and-dagger shenanigans?'

'Certainly, young Frank, but I'm afraid it's more of a historical interest than of any cogent use in the current conflict.'

'In that case,' said Babs, 'if it's not going to help us win the war, then I'm not interested. I'll leave you two to your esoteric sadness.'

'So what's this then?' asked Ledbetter, stabbing the parchment with a forefinger.

'That, Mr Ledbetter, is a two-thousand-year-old map of the area in question, drawn by no lesser person than Lucius Paulus.'

'Who in Lucifer's lantern is Lucius Paulus?'

'Only ancient Rome's most gifted civil engineer and designer.'

'Not much of a cartographer though, was he? Looks as if it was done by a four-year-old.'

'Bit crude, I'll grant you, but accurate enough to prove a point. Compare it to the first photo, what's missing?'

'Well, it's obvious – the area in question.'

'Exactly.'

'So put me out of my misery then. What is it?'

'Mine spoil.'

'Mine spoil! That's it?'

''Fraid so.'

'Seven square miles of mine spoil? Must have left one hell of a hole in the ground. By the way, what's the relevance of the second photo?'

'Take a look, would you?'

Ledbetter squinted through the magnifier. 'Looks like a road to me – what's the shaded series of rectangles at one end?'

'A town that's no longer there.'

'And why the sudden stop at the other end?'

'Don't know, but it ends at a small horseshoe-shaped hill.'

'Well, I can tell you this. Your horseshoe-shaped hill is not a result of anything natural – it's man-made.'

'No kidding?'

'Plain as the nose on your face.'

Covington was not about to argue with a man who had an unblemished record when it came to distinguishing between natural geography and a well-camouflaged gun emplacement. Ledbetter headed back to his desk. *He'll get about halfway*, Covington thought to himself.

Right on cue, Ledbetter wheeled around. 'Just a cotton pickin' minute, you think that hill is the entrance to the mine, don't you? And that Roman Brigadoon is where all the workers lived! Well, all I can say is that whatever they were mining must have been incredibly valuable to warrant shifting millions of tons of spoil into a heap the size of the Isle of Wight!'

Covington's smile gave Ledbetter his answer.

Covington remained behind after everyone had left that evening. He wanted to rectify something he'd overlooked. Since the parchment had been in his possession, he had not examined it closely under magnification. He slid the parchment under the magnifier. The possible entrance was parallel to the sea rather than facing it – so mine, not tunnel, was still the more likely. Covington was tired, and he wondered if his mind was playing tricks. He removed the magnifier and pulled a powerful magnifying glass from his draw. His eyes did not deceive him. There at the very end of the line on the French side, indicating the entrance to the tunnel, was a right angle, making the entrance parallel to the sea, not facing it. Lucius wanted to convince people it was a mine. He'd excavate about a hundred yards north-eastward, then turn ninety degrees to the north. Straight out under the Channel.

The next morning, Ledbetter made straight for Covington's desk.

'Ah, my noble Lord Covington,' he greeted, 'just to let you know that if you want any help with your "off piste" project, give me a shout.'

'Just a silly theory I'm working on, but thanks anyway. I will let you know.'

'Well, I'll tell you what I do know, your Lordship. That map you showed me was part of a larger one and I'll wager a fiver to one of my nose hairs that you know where the rest of it is! Oh, and one more thing, that huge forest that is marked on the map is not in the photo. Went the same way as Brigadoon, did it?'

Sitting in his digs that evening, Covington firmly admonished himself. He was getting carried away with this preposterous tunnel under the Channel theory, knowing full well that it would be a gargantuan task for 1940s machinery, let alone crude Roman hand tools. But his scientific mind was well-honed and he'd learned it was foolhardy to dismiss anything until proven one hundred percent wrong. After all, two thousand five hundred years before Caesar, the Egyptians had quarried, fashioned, transported and erected more than six million tons of granite to build the Great Pyramid of Giza. Perhaps he was looking at it through twentieth century eyes? The Roman army didn't have tanks, vehicles or artillery. It consisted of men with swords and spears. Therefore, a tunnel six-foot square would be sufficient, enough room for two men to march abreast. You could be putting five thousand men an hour on foreign soil. Moreover, the smaller the tunnel, the lesser the amount of spoil and the shorter time needed to dig it. He did a quick calculation in his head. A tunnel twenty-five miles long, two yards by two yards – that's one and three quarter million cubic yards of material to be shifted. Could an army of slave labour move that much hacked-out rock in three years? Very, very unlikely. *Get out of fantasy land while the getting's good*, he told himself. He satisfied himself with the theory that the massive spoil heap at Calais was a geographical freak and that Lucius had just humoured Caesar by starting and then abandoning the tunnel. One day, he would return to see just how far it had got.

However, he hadn't realised he'd lit the blue touch paper of the firework that was Frank Ledbetter, who came into work the next day positively fizzing.

A pea soup fog greeted Covington as he opened the door of his airfield digs, and he half walked, half groped his way across to the CIU building. No sooner had he entered than Ledbetter bounded across the room to meet him. But before a word could pass between them, Babs barked at them from her office, 'Oi, you two, Flanagan and Allen, in here.'

The pair sheepishly trudged into Babs' office and waited for the inevitable ticking off.

'I don't know what you two are up to, but I strongly suspect it has precious little to do with defeating Hitler. However, it has not gone unnoticed hereabouts that your contribution to the work we do has been nothing short of astonishing – above and beyond if you like.'

Covington and Ledbetter exchanged a playful grin. They knew they were good.

'But that does not give you the right to use office time and tools on some fanciful wild goose chase. You are both long overdue a rest and some leave. The fog is going to ground all our planes for at least the next two days. Now would be a good time to take it. So here's the deal, you have the next forty-eight hours to get this nonsense out of your system. All CIU equipment is at your disposal but if you use the phones, remember security protocols still apply.'

'Thanks, Babs,' they said in stereo.

Ledbetter was ready to go off like a shaken pop bottle but was halted in his tracks by Covington's raised hand.

'Me first, Frank, my train set.'

He relayed all his thoughts from the previous evening and just about every theory hit the buffers with a resounding wallop.

'OK,' said Ledbetter, 'let's use that as our starting point. I got in early this morning and pored over those aerials for ages. Your conclusions do concur with most of my findings.'

Covington nodded. 'Tell me what you know, Frank.'

'Well, your two-man tunnel theory makes sense – until you try and get rid of one point seven five million cubic yards of waste in short order, using not much more than wooden-wheeled donkey carts. I came at it from the other end, concentrating on our large area of spoil. I calculated its cubic capacity, and I'm here to tell you that if all that waste came from a tunnel dug under the Channel, it's a tunnel you could get the Queen Mary through.'

'So are you telling me it's not spoil at all?'

'It can't be, there's just too damn much of it.'

'You know what it is, don't you?'

'Well let's say I've got a better theory than your mate Juste.'

'His lines between fact and unproven seemed to be a bit blurred at times.'

'Do you mind if I contact some bods who could help?'

'And what's the particular area of expertise of these "bods"?'

'Ancient geology, and by ancient, we are talking back to continental drift.'

'Fine, but keep the tunnel thing under your hat. They may just recommend that we are both sectioned!'

Covington drove into work two days later, the sky gin-clear following seventy-two hours of heavy murk. A glum-looking Ledbetter was perched on Covington's desk.

'Methinks by your expression you are the bearer of bad tidings, young Frank.'

'No use calling it anything else.'

'So what conclusions did your esteemed colleagues come to?'

'Well, your friend Juste was right about one thing – where our spoil heap is now there once was a seaside cove. However, he was several million years out regarding when the infill occurred.'

'Perhaps something got lost in translation. His English was pidgin at best. And I take it by the timescale its transportation was not undertaken by human hand.'

'Something a bit more powerful – tectonics.'

'So what we have is something similar to an ice age moraine?'

Ledbetter nodded.

Covington paced about the room. 'Still doesn't explain the disappearing forest or the fact it's not on Lucius' map.'

'The brains trust did come up with a couple of theories. Lucius may just have had enough nous to know what the spoil heap was and was totally unsuitable for tunnelling through, so deliberately left it off the map.'

Covington shrugged in agreement. 'And most of Britain was covered with forest until it was hacked down wholesale to keep Britannia ruling the waves.'

He slowly stroked his chin. 'Do you buy it, Frank?'

'Not completely, no.'

'Neither do I, but I'm afraid any further investigation is going to have to wait until the war is won.'

'Indeed,' agreed Ledbetter. 'Speaking of which, we'd better get back to playing our part in the aforementioned victory before Babs has our guts for garters.'

– CHAPTER SIX –

Wednesday, August 23rd, 1944, Cabinet War Rooms, London, England.

The team at the Central Interpretation Unit were making about as much headway as the invasion force in France. Photo reconnaissance Spitfires and Mosquitoes flew sortie after sortie over Northern France and every print told the same story of enemy consolidation. The forlorn hope that the Germans might need to move men and materiel to the Eastern Front to confront the Russian advance came to nothing as the Soviet armies were as bogged down as the Allies were.

A very concerned Prime Minister Churchill convened an urgent summit at Number Ten with all the Allied top brass in attendance. After an hour of heated debate, precious little in the way of possible solutions had been submitted.

Churchill crossed his arms on the desk in front of him, leaned forward and peered menacingly over the top of his spectacles. 'Gentlemen, I don't need to stress the severity of the situation we find ourselves in. If we don't break this deadlock, and soon, the consequences will be too dire to contemplate.'

General Eisenhower, commander-in-chief of the Allied Forces, felt obliged to comment. 'Mr Prime Minister, the way I see it is we somehow have to split the German defences. There's one thing in our favour. They have put all their eggs in one basket by keeping us bottled up in Normandy. They're pretty thin on the ground in the rest of the Western theatre. Our problem is that the tactic is working.'

Churchill nodded sagely. 'Would I be right in thinking that the objective is to try and find a way to force the Germans to relocate a large portion of their forces in Normandy?'

'That's about the size of it, sir.'

'So, General, to compel the Germans into complying with our wishes, are we talking about launching a second invasion at a location well away from Normandy?'

'Can't see any other way, sir.'

'And its chances of success, General?'

'If we can limit the U-boat damage and get the force ashore before the Normandy defence force gets there, it could be possible, but I'm not going to dress it up, sir, the smart money would be on failure.'

Churchill leaned back in his chair, placed both hands behind his head and gently exhaled, 'It may be a long shot that we are forced into playing.'

Sitting at the furthest end of the Cabinet table, drawing gently on his pipe, was Commander Bushell. He had not uttered one word during the whole meeting. Apart from Churchill, no one had a clue who he was. When Churchill ran through an introductory role call at the start of proceedings, he had simply been introduced as 'Commander Bushell' and nobody thought anything more of it.

Bushell spoke for the first time. 'Do I deduce that if enough German forces could be persuaded to leave the area, then Allied progress into France would resume and be successful?' he asked, exuding a billow of blue smoke.

After a cursory glance at one another, Eisenhower spoke on the assembly's behalf. 'There are no cast-iron guarantees in warfare, Commander, but I'd say with a fair wind, that would be the case. However, if the second invasion was decimated, we'd soon be back to square one with a large chunk of our reinforcements now gone.'

Bushell shrugged. 'In that case, why not just hoodwink the Germans into thinking there's going to be a second invasion?'

Mutters of disbelief filled the room.

Bushell attempted appeasement. 'Gentlemen,' he reasoned, 'we successfully convinced the Germans D-Day was going to make landfall at Calais, and with the help of a cadaver whose pockets were brimming with false information, the Germans mobilised a huge force to meet an invasion of Greece, when our true target was Sicily.'

Churchill deemed it was time for an introduction.

'This gentleman is Commander Peter Bushell. He's here on behalf of the Combined Intelligence Committee. What Peter doesn't know about skulduggery, deception and generally being underhand isn't worth knowing.'

Bushell nodded and smiled in acknowledgement of the back-handed compliment.

'Do you have anything in mind, Commander?' asked Eisenhower.

'I have the seed of an idea, General.'

'Then can I suggest, Prime Minister, that the commander proceeds with all haste to transform this seed into a full-grown plant? Meantime, I think an invasion force should be assembled as soon as possible, in case subterfuge fails.'

'If you're going to sell the idea of an invasion, then mustering the force would have to be part of the deception in any event,' explained Bushell. 'So we would be, in effect, killing two birds with one stone. May I suggest Kent as a good place?'

'Peter, I know you of old,' said Churchill with a smile. 'You already have something up your sleeve, don't you? Don't tell me anything else yet – it's probably so preposterous I would think I'd need my head examining letting you have your way. General, commence forthwith assembling your invasion force in Kent. It'll give the German intelligence here something to report. We meet again in two weeks.'

Bushell raised his hand. 'Just one more thing, Prime Minister. Could I have your permission to filch two Cambridge grads from the Central Interpretation Unit?'

'Filch away,' said Churchill with a wave of his arm.

– CHAPTER SEVEN –

Thursday, August 24th, 1944, RAF Medmenham,
Buckinghamshire, England.

Babs poked her head around her office door, waited for Covington and Ledbetter to catch her eye, and beckoned them with her right forefinger.

'Come in,' she invited, 'and shut the door behind you.'

Jack and Frank exchanged a glance, the same thought passing through their heads. *Are we in trouble again?*

Babs detected the concern. 'Don't worry, you haven't done anything wrong. Well, not that I know of anyway. You two jokers are going to London. The Combined Intelligence Committee wishes to see you. A car will be here to pick you up in two hours. This gives you roughly one hour to go home, collect your belongings and return here.'

'The dirty tricks department? Why on earth would they want to see us?' Covington asked.

Babs shrugged. 'No idea.' The hint of a smile told Jack and Frank that this wasn't strictly true.

Ledbetter pleaded, 'Can't you tell us anything, Babs?'

'Not really, no.'

'Can't or won't?'

Another tell-tale smile. Babs was loving this – and she made them wait for her reply. 'Jack, you may want to take the file you have at home on that two-day wild goose chase you went on last year. You also have a large envelope in your bottom right-hand desk drawer. It's full of aerials you've copied that you think I don't know about. You know, the ones relating to the Roman tunnel? Take those as well.'

'But no one knows about that.'

Babs guffawed. 'Oh, come on, boys – really? You work in intelligence, albeit photographic interpretation. Every damn word said and action taken in this place is scrutinised, analysed and generally gone over with a fine toothcomb.'

Babs leaned forward on her desk, the smile replaced by a stern stare. 'I will tell you this. My gut feeling is that this is top-drawer important. We could even be talking outcome of the war stuff. Give it your best shot, boys, and good luck.'

By mid-afternoon, Covington and Ledbetter were sat outside an office deep in the bowels of the Admiralty Building. The almost black floor-to-ceiling teak panelling gave the corridor a sinister feel, which the sparsely spaced forty-watt bulbs did little to alleviate.

'God, it's like being in a giant coffin,' observed Ledbetter.

Covington agreed. 'I swear the place went darker when they put the lights on.'

A lackey squeaked down the corridor and approached them. 'Lord Covington? Frank Ledbetter?'

Both acknowledged their identity.

'Commander Bushell will see you now.'

Peter St John Montague Bushell could best be summed up by a footnote in his last report from Winchester College. The axiom – *there is a fine line between genius and madness* – could well have been created for Peter. He wrote his first detective novel at eighteen, was prematurely bald by twenty-four, and he considered he was having a bad day if it took longer than twenty minutes to complete *The Times* crossword. Just too young to fight in the Great War, he went to Oxford in 1919 and studied the eccentric combination of English and Physics. He got firsts in both.

Following the post mortem on the war, both government and military came to two major conclusions. First rate intelligence enhanced the odds of victory considerably and feeding false intelligence to the enemy achieved even better results. Striking while the iron was hot, the Office of Naval Intelligence was soon set up to work alongside other secret services, with a brief to concentrate on the misinformation side.

The ONI scoured the Oxbridge colleges for suitable talent and it wasn't long before they tracked down Bushell. He reached the rank of commander by the time war broke out in 1939 and contributed hugely to Operation Mincemeat. Many of the ruses that fooled the Germans into thinking the second front was going to land at Calais had been down to Bushell.

He ushered Covington and Ledbetter into his office with open arms. 'Gentlemen, welcome, please take a seat. Good of you to come so soon and apologies for all the cloak and dagger stuff.'

He pressed an intercom button. 'Lieutenant

Parkinson, could you bring in three cups of tea, and see if you can't rustle up a biscuit or two? We're pretty informal down here in this rabbit warren, and as you two are still technically civilians, I'll call you Jack and Frank if that's OK. By the way, Jack, I hope an old Etonian doesn't mind having a Wykehamist* as a boss?'

'I'll make allowances,' said Covington affably.

'Right, to work, gentlemen. Your Roman tunnel. I've been given the briefest outline of your voyage into what may or may not be Roman mythology, but I want you to expand on your theories at every juncture. Do not omit anything. Ah, tea!' A slim, well-starched Wren entered with a tray bearing three cups of Earl Grey and a plate of digestives.

Covington and Ledbetter spent the next hour taking Bushell through a journey in time, explaining what they thought was possible evidence and what they'd dismissed as dead ends. They laid out before him the maps – both ancient and modern – and all the aerial photographs, pointing out what they thought were geographic anomalies in the prints.

Bushell slowly lifted his pipe to his lips, applied a match to the bowl, took three huge puffs and waved away the excess smoke with a flap of his hand.

'I have two questions for you. Do you think this tunnel could possibly exist and, on a scale of one to ten, what are the odds of its existence?'

Covington puffed out his cheeks. 'I haven't dismissed the idea of its existence, but I don't want to over-sell it, so I'll give it a one. Frank?'

Ledbetter rubbed his chin. 'Depends on what you call its existence. That plans were drawn up for it, say six. We have pretty solid evidence for that. That a lip service start

35

was made on it, I'd say four. And it probably didn't get any further than fifty yards? Probably less than a half.'

'Splendid!' Bushell exclaimed.

The pair were slightly surprised at his reaction. They both thought their answers would have rendered whatever he had in mind a non-starter.

Bushell had noticed their shock. 'Ah! explanation necessary! You see, gentlemen, the art of subterfuge is not making your target believe something, but making them *want* to believe it. You tell them the answer before you ask the question, no matter how fanciful the answer is. It's like a lengthy dance of the seven veils, but the veils number a lot more than seven. You two have not dismissed the possibility of this tunnel's existence, based upon the evidence you have thus far gleaned. Through our various nefarious channels, we can let the Germans know that there is evidence of a tunnel beneath the Channel, excavated by the Romans, and that the Allies intend to use it to land troops on French soil. Remember, all the Western nations are fully aware of Roman engineering capabilities – even if they didn't extend to digging twenty-mile-long undersea tunnels. If we make them *want* to believe it, it will cause their eyes to light up, having visions of lying in wait and knocking off the hapless Allied force as they emerge. We will then embellish the ruse by giving them a steady drip, drip of evidence – which, by the way, will include massing troops in Kent, and that will not go unnoticed by German informers – and that's where you two come in. Between us, we have to convince them. My team will try and persuade the Germans that the massive mustering of men and materiel in southern Kent is there to cross the Channel below, rather than above or on the ocean waves.

You two will be the temptresses feeding the Germans tasty titbits compiled from your research and presented convincingly and believably. Would that be beyond your capabilities?'

'I think we'd both like a shot at it, sir,' said Covington. 'Where and when do we start?'

'Tomorrow morning, nine o'clock, the office next door. Lieutenant Parkinson will show you to your hotel – it's just around the corner. Spend the evening kicking around some ideas and we'll meet first thing. Don't run up too big a bar tab, will you?'

Wykehamist – ex pupil of Winchester college.

– CHAPTER EIGHT –

Friday, August 25th, 1944, the Admiralty Building, London, England.

Covington and Ledbetter, having been issued with new Admiralty passes, were escorted by a wren through the maze of corridors to their new office, where Commander Bushell was waiting for them.

'Welcome, gentlemen,' said Bushell, proffering his hand. 'Let's make a start. What are your initial thoughts?'

'Well,' said Covington, 'even the dopiest German isn't going to believe we can get enough men and materiel through a narrow tunnel quickly enough to open a third front before being discovered.'

Bushell nodded his approval. 'I like the way your minds are working. We'll make con men of you yet. Please continue.'

'We think we need to convince the Germans that it's going to be a three-pronged attack. They must believe that a unit – just strong enough to take out the shore batteries from behind – would be sent through the tunnel. Alongside this, a parachute drop would occupy German forces, allowing the tunnel force a clear run at the shore batteries. With German AA guns occupying the south, a parachute drop into Calais would not be complete suicide. Lastly, the main force could cross the Channel. I think the Germans would believe this.'

'Splendid!' Bushell exclaimed. 'And you may have unknowingly passed your first test in underhand mind games.'

Covington and Ledbetter looked quizzically at Bushell.

'Gentlemen, what is our job?'

'To make the Germans think there's a tunnel,' ventured Ledbetter. Then it dawned on him. He leapt to his feet. 'And this plan does not work if they don't think there's a tunnel!'

'Of course!' Covington chimed in. 'Without the tunnel, the plan would sound like a not very believable hoax, but with the tunnel, just plausible enough to be believable!'

'Exactly! But don't forget, gentlemen, this is the easy bit, and through various nefarious channels, we can let the Germans know of our plan. The hard bit is convincing the Germans that this tunnel exists, or at least making them believe it *might*. They know we are desperate, fighting against the clock. Thereby willing to try desperate measures. They also know that in this conflict we have a track record of making the fanciful work. So, by the end of the week, do you think you can come up with a plan of action that will sow the seeds of this deception?'

The pair nodded in unison.

'Good. We'll call it Operation Auger.'

'Appropriate,' said Ledbetter with a grin.

After lunch on the Friday, Covington and Ledbetter sat nervously in their office awaiting the arrival of Bushell, both hoping they were not going to disappoint the commander.

Bushell breezed in, gestured for them both to be seated and said in his usual kindly manner, 'Right, gentlemen, what have you got for me?'

Covington began, 'Right, sir, as a matter of urgency, do you think it would be possible to assemble a large fleet of earth-moving equipment, lorries and everything else that goes with a large civil engineering project and get them toot suite somewhere close to Dover?'

'And then?' asked Bushell.

'Point them towards France and start digging. A tunnel has to have two ends and we need to fool the Germans into thinking that we are looking for the entrance at our end.'

'Indeed,' agreed Bushell. 'I will mobilise the vast resources at my disposal and the first sod will be removed before sparrow chirp on Monday. We need to get the balance just right. Make a good fist of trying to disguise what we are up to, so the Germans think we are up to no good, but be just slip-shod enough to allow them to find out about it. If enemy photo-reconnaissance is up to snuff, then the first evidence of our excavations will be on a desk at the Abwehr* before close of play on Wednesday.'

'What if their PR plane kite gets shot down?' asked Ledbetter.

Bushell shook his head. 'Oh, it won't. The RAF attack any PR planes they see – the Germans would be suspicious if they didn't – but the pilots are under orders to miss.'

Covington smiled. 'Boy, am I glad you are on our side!'

'Right,' said Ledbetter firmly, 'by the middle of next week, the Germans will know we are up to something in Kent, and coupled with the troop buildup there, their inquisitiveness quotient will be off the scale. They will have no idea what we are digging for, and no clue if or how it is in any way connected to the troop buildup.'

A pregnant silence filled the office. All three knew that now was the time for believable flesh to be put on the bones of the German investigation.

Covington broke the ice. 'Commander, would it be possible to track down someone in Paris?'

Covington already knew the answer. The pair of them had ceased to be amazed by Bushell's capabilities. Even the fact that he seemed to know everything about everyone didn't unduly worry them anymore. They had initially regarded the sign on his desk that read 'I can do the difficult today, you'll have to wait till the end of the week for the impossible' as something amusing to put visitors at ease. The pair now saw it as a believable mission statement.

'I'm sure that's possible,' Bushell answered. 'Who are we talking about?'

'Didier Pascal, he's the—'

Bushell finished Covington's sentence for him, '…the Paris museum curator.'

'Exactly,' Covington confirmed, 'but he may no longer be in Paris. He may even be dead.'

Bushell shook his head. 'Generally speaking, the Nazis usually leave academics who can't contribute to their war machine alone. People like museum bods, for instance. If he were a doctor or a scientist or mathematician, then it would be a different story. So as long as he's not Jewish or has been killed, there's a good chance he's still working at the museum. The Germans are a very cultural nation and are always keen to demonstrate it. The chances are the museum is still open for business.'

'He's going to be a very important link in this chain. We are back to square one if we can't use him.'

'He could be vital,' agreed Bushell. 'We'll use the resistance to contact him rather than an agent. They'll know the lay of the land better and, of course, they will be in a better position to know if he's batting for the home team, as it were.'

'Will it take long?' Ledbetter enquired.

Bushell shook his head. 'Now we have a good foothold in France, communications between London and Paris are a good deal easier. Forty-eight hours at most, probably sooner.'

'The Germans are going to need a bit more than historical hearsay and a few spurious holes in the Kent countryside for them to take the bait,' Ledbetter pointed out. 'We will need Lucius Paulus' parchment map, plus our aerials to fall into German hands.'

'True,' concurred Bushell. 'But the aerials could give the game away. How accurate is the parchment map? Does it give the exact location of the tunnel entrance?'

Covington shook his head. 'Map drawing was not an exact science in 57 BC. At best you can decipher that it's a map of the wider Calais area.'

'Good. You see, gentlemen, at the risk of repeating myself, timing is of the essence. Remember, the object of the exercise is to make the Germans move men and materiel from positions where it is holding up our advance and send them to the Calais area to meet Auger head-on. The Germans need to be convinced that Auger is happening long enough to do this, but too much prior notice might enable them to find the exact location of your horseshoe-shaped Roman excavation. A few hours of work with a couple of large earth movers would prove the non-existence of the tunnel and Auger would be dead in the water.'

'So what's our next move, Commander?'

'Well, I think it's time to let the Germans in on our little plan.'

Covington and Ledbetter looked at one another, then at Bushell.

Bushell read the look. 'And you two would like to know how? Simple. We code messages in several different ways. It keeps the Germans guessing. Anything we want the Germans to find out, we send via a code that we know the Germans have cracked. So, later this afternoon I will send a message to a mythical general saying nothing more than Operation Auger has been initiated. On Tuesday, one of our double agents will inform his controller of the troop build up and that the new excavations in Kent are connected to Operation Auger, but how or why is not known. That should prick up a few ears at the Abwehr!'

'Meanwhile, we have to find a way of persuading the Germans that the vital part of Auger is the fanciful existence of a two thousand-year-old tunnel,' Ledbetter pointed out.

Bushel smiled and corrected him. 'Not fanciful, Frank, possible. Gentlemen, a week on Monday we'll have a meeting with the prime minister and all the heads of Allied High Command. By then the plans for Auger need to be complete and ready for implementation, so we have a busy few days in front of us. Can I suggest we meet here on Sunday morning?'

Abwehr - German counter-intelligence.

– CHAPTER NINE –

Friday, August 25th, 1944, Abwehr HQ, Berlin, Germany.

Oberst Dieter Vilma joined the Abwehr, albeit reluctantly, straight from Heidelberg University in 1940. The Abwehr had been continually trawling the universities for potential recruits since the end of the Great War, despite the Versailles treaty forbidding them to have a secret service. Students with exceptional skills in Maths and English were particularly prized. Vilma was about to embark on his doctorate in advanced mathematics when he came to the notice of the Abwehr, and when they learned that he was also a chess grandmaster at nineteen, his contribution to the Third Reich was rubber-stamped. Vilma was far from being a rabid Nazi and regarded himself to be too mild-mannered and lacking the deviousness for counterintelligence. But it was better than any military alternative, so with some misgivings, he found himself behind a desk at 76 Tirpitzufer, the HQ of the Abwehr.

Vilmer methodically tapped a pencil against his teeth while studying the latest communication from

Snapdragon. Snapdragon was the codename of one of the few remaining German agents left in England and Vilmer had his suspicions that he was either a double agent or the British knew exactly who he was. (It was the former that was true and British intelligence was feeding the Germans a steady diet of misinformation via Snapdragon, knowing full well that it would land on one desk or another at Abwehr HQ.)

Vilma stared at a short message about the continuing buildup of troops and supplies massing in the southeast of England. German air reconnaissance had been reporting this for weeks. It was old news and Vilma was pondering if it was worth passing on to the commander when his second-in-command, Hauptmann Max Bierhoff, arrived bearing two mugs of coffee.

Max Bierhoff's military career had ended after sustaining a severe injury during the invasion of France, having been a distinguished soldier since joining the Wehrmacht from officer training school in 1939. No longer fit enough to be on active service, he was transferred to the Abwehr to give a military perspective on what the Allies' next move might be.

'You are looking very thoughtful, Herr Oberst,' said Bierhoff.

Vilmer nodded. 'I'm puzzled, Max. Why are the Allies being so overt in massing troops in Kent and the surrounding area? They surely can't think we'll be fooled twice, making out that they are going to land in one place when the intention is to land somewhere else?'

'It doesn't take a military genius, Herr Oberst. They are trying to make us think that they are going to send a second invasion force across the Channel to land somewhere between Dieppe and Dunkirk and are hoping we will move our precious defences that are holding up the Allied advance in the south to meet this new threat. The Allies also know that this time we will be ready for them. Even if they succeed, the losses would be unacceptably high. They know this, we know this, hence the stalemate.'

Vilma eased back in his chair and aimed his pencil at Bierhoff. 'So who's going to blink first, Max?'

'It's a race against time, Herr Oberst. We need time to further develop vengeance weapons. The Allies want to deny us that time before we can do so. The only way to achieve our goals is by pressing on towards the Fatherland. The longer the stalemate, the more it favours us.'

'So when and where, Max?' Vilma asked, semi-rhetorically.

'Time is against them, Herr Oberst, for the reason I've just explained, and as we head into autumn, every day there is less daylight, not to mention the onset of winter storms. My best guess is sometime in the next five to six weeks, landing in an arc no more than thirty-five miles from Dover, trying to overwhelm us with sheer numbers.'

'I see,' mused Vilma.

'You don't seem convinced, Herr Oberst.'

'Do you play chess, Max?'

'I know the moves, Herr Oberst. No more than that.'

'There's a high risk-high reward strategy called the Rubliov gambit. You make several very unsubtle attacking moves, making your opponent set a trap for you. Just when he thinks he has you, you make an unexpected move from left field, completely wrong-footing him.'

'And you think that is what is happening here?'

'I don't know, Max. I just don't know.'

– CHAPTER TEN –

Sunday, August 27th, 1944, the Admiralty Building, London, England.

Bushell was sitting on the corner of the desk in their office, half-hidden by a haze of smoke from his pipe when Covington and Ledbetter rolled in just before nine. He rose to greet them, dispersing the fug as he did so.

'Good morning, gentlemen. Great news!' he said jovially. 'The resistance has tracked down Didier Pascal!'

'I take it he's still alive then,' said Covington with a smile.

'He is indeed!' Bushell affirmed. 'And he still works at the museum, albeit part-time and unpaid. But the best news is, he's not a member of the resistance.'

'And how is that good news?' Ledbetter queried.

'Well, if he doesn't know anything, he can't tell the Germans anything, can he?'

Not for the first time, Bushell gazed upon puzzled expressions.

'I thought the idea was that we wanted him to give the Germans info?' Covington reasoned.

'In this case, not divulging information, but simply telling the truth – well, sort of. To begin with, German intelligence in Paris is reasonably good. They will have a fair idea that Didier is not a resistance member and thereby will trust him. The resistance will deliver the map and warn Didier to expect a visit from those nice German secret service men, telling him to just recount his and your visit to the Calais countryside in 1939 and explain why you were there – with just a couple of white lies.'

'Which are?' asked Covington.

'One, the map never came to England. It's been in the Paris museum since your expedition was cut short by the war, and two, the aforementioned sudden end to your searches happened before you were able to discover any concrete evidence, including any possible entrance.'

'Will that be enough to convince the Germans that a tunnel just might exist?'

'In itself, no. But remember what I told you, make them *want* to believe it. The Germans will no doubt do a check on you, Jack, and find out that you are an eminent Cambridge graduate and a leading world expert on the Roman Empire. Didier will tell them about the forest and the town that used to be there, as well as the theory of why they were there – and the snowball will slowly roll down the hill.'

'So how do the Germans discover that Didier is a man worth talking to?'

'Because I shall tell them,' said Bushell with a smirk. 'Not in so many words, of course, just a couple of gentle pointers.'

Ledbetter shook his head. 'Call me a sceptic, Commander, but if I were a German, I would still be a long way from convinced.'

'Your scepticism is well founded, Frank, but I've not yet finished. Didier will be encouraged to tell his questioners that there's a raft of other evidence – maps, photos, geographic anomalies, all of which is in your hands, Jack. With this being five years ago, Didier can be pretty vague about the evidence and blame it on the passage of time. And the beauty of it, it's all true – and nothing is more plausible than the actual truth.'

Covington shot up from his chair. 'Problem, Commander. Juste Gilbert. Didier will tell them about Juste and if they track him down, he knows where all these places are.'

'Of course Didier will tell them about Juste. We are relying on it. This gives the story more credibility. But what Didier and the Germans don't know is that Juste Gilbert was killed in a bombing raid in 1940. I'm sorry, Jack, but it is to our advantage.'

Covington shrugged. 'Calais was heavily bombed, not everyone would have survived. Any other snippet, Commander?'

'I do have a couple more convincers, yes. They will get to know that you two worked for the Central Interpretation Unit.'

'And we all know how they will get to know,' said Ledbetter ruefully.

Bushell smiled and shrugged, acknowledging the playful dig.

He continued, 'The fact that you worked there won't raise any German eyebrows – perfectly realistic work for people with your sort of knowledge and qualifications. They will also discover that you are no longer employed there and that you are now seconded to the army stationed in Kent.'

Not for the first time, Covington and Ledbetter stared blankly at each other.

'Do you take particular delight in confusing us, Commander?' asked Ledbetter.

'Yes, I'm aware that you're in a room deep under the streets of London and not in a field in Kent. The Germans mustn't discover that you work here. If they do they'd soon put two and two together – the two foremost experts on this under-Channel tunnel both working for the secret service? It would scream "scam" from the rooftops. So even as we speak, two of our agents are observing with wonderfully feigned interest the ground being excavated in a Kentish field, supposedly assisting in the hunt for a mythical tunnel.'

'They wouldn't be named Jack Covington and Frank Ledbetter, would they?'

'That's what it says in the register of a hotel just outside Dover,' agreed Bushell. 'Since you two have always been civilian workers, it makes you more anonymous than if you were military. Nobody outside of anyone who knows you has a clue what you look like.'

'And if there just happens to be some German-friendly lugholes earwigging, no doubt our two doppelgangers will not be too observant of the careless talk rules when chatting in the hotel bar after a day tramping around in our newly dug hole,' Covington deduced.

Bushell's grin gave him his answer.

– CHAPTER ELEVEN –

Tuesday, August 29th, 1944, Abwehr HQ, Berlin, Germany.

Oberst Vilma lowered himself wearily into his chair to begin yet another day of wading through a mountain of information, the vast majority of which was going to be either useless or irrelevant. He wondered about the outcome of the war. Like most Germans, he expected D-Day to be the beginning of the end, and it would be just a matter of time before the Reich capitulated. But the unexpected hiatus in Normandy and the talk of game-changing new weapons had caused everyone to re-think. Vilma rejected the tack taken by the more fanatical Nazis who expected nothing less than a total and glorious victory – that was for the birds. But Vilma believed if the stalemate were to continue for another couple of months, then it was not beyond the bounds of possibility that maybe, just maybe, Germany could sue for favourable peace terms without a single foreign boot desecrating German soil. His reasoning was interrupted by Hauptmann Bierhoff bearing a raft of papers.

'The latest updates about the mustering of troops and supplies in Kent Herr Oberst.'

'Any developments, Max?'

'Yes, Herr Oberst, something quite strange. For some reason, the Allies have begun excavating in fields near Dover on quite a large scale, an area of about six hectares.'

'Any theories?'

'Could be an opencast mine, Herr Oberst. We know there's a lot of coal in Kent.'

Vilma stretched his legs out under the desk and stared up at the ceiling. Slowly, he leaned forward and shook his head.

'You seem unconvinced, Herr Oberst.'

'How far from these new army camps is all this digging taking place, Max?'

'Right slap bang in the middle of them, Herr Oberst.'

'The Allies are assembling a massive army, together with all the accompanying vehicles and supplies, and they start digging for coal right in the middle of the whole shooting match? Rather odd, don't you think?'

'Well, now you come to mention it, Herr Oberst.'

'Get on to air reconnaissance. Ask them to get as many snaps as they dare. There's something fishy about this.'

'Right away, Herr Oberst.'

Bierhoff headed for the door.

'Wait, Max, wait.'

'Herr Oberst?'

'Tell them to do it Thursday. Let them have a couple of days to develop the site, then the photos may tell us more.'

'Very well, Herr Oberst.'

Bierhoff exited the room but was met in the doorway by an office junior. She handed him a note. Bierhoff read it and his eyes widened.

'Looks important, Max,' said Vilma, stretching out his hand.

Bierhoff hurried over to the desk and handed Vilma the single sheet of paper.

'It's from Snapdragon, Herr Oberst.'

Vilma took less than ten seconds to read it.

'So our number one agent in England has discovered something called "Operation Auger" but has no idea what it is.'

'But he does say some of the highest ranking officials in British intelligence are involved with it, Herr Oberst,' Bierhoff reasoned.

Vilma nodded. 'Which means we have to take it seriously, Max. Message an acknowledgement to Snapdragon, tell him to investigate further and keep us updated.'

By four that afternoon, Vilma had run out of steam and was contemplating an early finish and heading for home, followed by a bath, some schnapps and an early night. He stood up, stretched, and was heading for the coat stand when Bierhoff appeared in the doorway with the inevitable piece of paper. Vilma sighed his disappointment.

'An update from Snapdragon, Herr Oberst.'

'And what's he uncovered?'

Instead of answering, Bierhoff let Vilma scan the note.

'We were right, Max. There could be more to these excavations than meets the eye.'

'It appears so, Herr Oberst.'

'So Snapdragon thinks that the mass gathering of these troops in Kent is part of this "Operation Auger". Is he aware of all this digging that is going on?'

'I don't think so, Herr Oberst. Otherwise, he would have mentioned it.'

Vilma swivelled his chair around to face the huge map of Britain behind him. 'Where exactly is Snapdragon based, Max?'

'Just south of London, Herr Oberst, a small town called Mettlesham in the county of Surrey. His cover is a sales rep for a factory making work clothes. It allows him the freedom to travel.'

Bierhoff indicated the town with a pencil and Vilma marked it with a drawing pin.

'Kent is not too far from Surrey.'

'The two counties border one another, Herr Oberst,' Bierhoff confirmed.

'In that case, get back to Snapdragon, tell him to head for Dover immediately, and have a poke around to see what he can uncover. No more than two days and have him report back by Thursday. We'll then compile a report and send it upstairs.'

'Very well, Herr Oberst.'

'Oh, and Max…'

'Herr Oberst?'

'Don't mention the excavations to Snapdragon. Let him discover a connection if there is one.'

'As you say, Herr Oberst. I'll get on to Snapdragon immediately.'

Just before reaching the door, Bierhoff half-turned, looked at his feet and then at Vilma.

'Herr Oberst, may I speak freely?'

'Of course, Max, what is troubling you?'

'Do you have your suspicions about Snapdragon, Herr Oberst?'

Vilma's lips tightened and he slowly looked up at Bierhoff.

'You have worked here almost as long as I have, Max.

It breeds cynicism and mistrust that gets to us all. You become so psychotically suspicious to the point where you don't trust your own shadow. If I'm not one hundred per cent sure of Snapdragon, then I have to say it is based on no evidence whatsoever. But there's something, just something, I have no idea what, that's telling me to be aware. It's odds-on I'm over-reacting though.'

Bierhoff slowly nodded and once again turned for the door.

'Max, let's try and keep each other sane.'

Despite the difference in their backgrounds and rank, the two had become good friends. Bierhoff smiled and left.

– CHAPTER TWELVE –

Wednesday, 30ᵗʰ August, 1944, the Admiralty Building, London, England.

Covington and Ledbetter were now familiar with the labyrinth that was the Admiralty Building. They could now make their way to their office without getting lost or needing to ask the way.

As expected, Bushell was waiting for them in their office. 'Morning, gentlemen,' he said in his usual genial manner. 'Let me start by bringing you up to speed. The Germans now know about Operation Auger and have suspicions that heavy machinery activity is going on. One must assume that they are keen to find out more about this. They've dispatched an agent to Dover to find out more. He's a double agent who works for us. His German codename is Snapdragon.'

'And where do we come in?' asked Frank.

'All in good time, all in good time. You two have one job to complete this morning before we move on to more serious matters. We have to formulate a tangible plan for Operation Auger. Despite what you might think, I can't do whatever I please. I am not God.'

Ledbetter guffawed; he was far from convinced.

Bushell continued. 'We've taken this deception as far as we safely can. Our next stop is the Cabinet War Rooms on Monday. So, between now and then, we need to knock our plans for Auger into shape – and they must be comprehensive in every detail. Comments?'

A short silence ensued; there was a lot to take in.

Both men started to speak at the same time.

'After you, Jack,' Ledbetter invited.

'Thanks, Frank. It seems to me that the timing is crucial. The high-ups must follow our lead. Is this possible?'

'Yes, it is,' Bushell agreed. 'Weather notwithstanding, of course.'

'So working backwards, as it were. Leading up to the starting gun,' Ledbetter said. 'It's our job to feed the Germans just enough info about the tunnel to make it believable, but not to give them enough time to do research. We don't want them to discover that it's a load of hogwash.'

'Yes, and as you say, timing is crucial,' Bushell concurred. 'We can control the narrative about the tunnel, but things could go all pear-shaped when the Germans visit Didier Pascal about the parchment map.'

'That's true, but there's also another thing...' Covington observed. 'We might need to postpone the whole thing if the weather goes against us.'

'We can't do that. The information will be out there and all will be lost,' said Jack.

Covington nodded. 'Agreed, but if truth be told, the weather isn't quite as important as it was for D-Day. It doesn't matter if it's a force ten gale or a flat calm. The invasion's true destination is Normandy, not Calais. This is just to buy us some time.'

The intercom flashed.

'Yes, Lieutenant.'

'Your visitor is here, Commander.'

'Good, send him in, will you? This concerns you two – the little job I mentioned earlier.'

There was a polite knock, and a small, wiry, middle-aged man joined them. He was warmly greeted by Bushell.

'Gentlemen,' Bushell enthused, 'let me introduce you to Snapdragon. You'll forgive me if I don't tell you his real name.'

Covington and Ledbetter couldn't have been more stunned if they had been introduced to Hitler himself. This was a bonafide secret service field agent, but, strangely, he looked so unlike a spy.

Covington was the first to recover his composure, proffering his hand. He noticed the top half of the agent's little finger on his right hand was missing.

'Pardon me, sir. Aren't you supposed to be in Kent, meeting our alter egos?'

'Why meet stand-ins when he can speak to the real McCoy?' replied Bushell.

'Should I assume that the other Jack and Frank don't exist, and are not in Kent?' asked a puzzled Ledbetter.

'Oh, they do exist and they are there. No one in this department, least of all me, thinks they're omniscient. We're happy to concede that there are probably a few German agents over here that we're unaware of. And it's likely that these agents already know about Auger. We must cover all bases. You both need to brief Snapdragon on the whys and wherefores of Roman tunnels. Arguments for and against.'

Covington and Ledbetter both looked on with a

mixture of awe and perplexity, not sure how to take Snapdragon.

Snapdragon spotted the awkwardness in them and sought to put them at their ease. 'All I need is a crash course,' he said. 'It's my job to make it believable to the Germans.'

Ledbetter was placated. 'Can we call you Snappy for short?' he said, giving him a friendly tap on the shoulder.

The tension dissipated as Covington and Ledbetter spent the next hour appraising Snapdragon of their findings. He seemed very happy with what he'd learned and was confident of being able to sell it to the Germans. They bade him farewell and Ledbetter wondered if they would ever meet again. They deemed it unlikely.

Bushell slapped the desk with his right hand. 'Right,' he barked. 'Now the real work begins…'

– CHAPTER THIRTEEN –

Thursday, August 31st, 1944, Abwehr HQ, Berlin, Germany.

Vilma sighed irritably and locked his hands behind his head. He'd been waiting impatiently all morning for updates on Operation Auger. He was unaware that a heavy bombing raid the previous night had delayed incoming communications, and messages were being delivered by motorcycle couriers from unharmed radio stations. At three o'clock Bierhoff strode in with a fistful of papers.

'What have we got, Max?'

'Virtually all relating to Auger, Herr Oberst.'

Bierhoff turned to leave.

'No, please stay, Max. Might be a case of two heads being better than one here.'

'Of course, Herr Oberst.'

The source of messages being detected was at its greatest during transmission, so they were kept as short as possible – although in this case, of course, it didn't matter. The British knew who was sending them, but the pretence had to be kept up. It therefore didn't take long to read all the posts from Snapdragon, and having done so, Vilma was a little less sceptical.

'Snapdragon has discovered all the excavating that's going on. He says it's more than probable that it's connected to both the troop buildup and Auger. We can therefore dismiss an opencast mine – unless, of course, the Allies intend to cross the Channel by steam train.'

'Quite so, Herr Oberst.'

'I do find the presence of these two civilians interesting though. Particularly as one of them is an English aristocrat – a Lord Covington and his partner, one Frank Ledbetter. The more we can find out about these two, the more we will learn about Auger.'

'I've checked through our records, Herr Oberst, and we have nothing on either. That's not surprising though. They are two civilians who appear to have no connection to the military.'

'What we need to do is find out their area of expertise. If we can work that out, then we can ascertain what they are doing in Kent. Hang on, you said that one of them is a lord of the realm?'

'Affirmative, Herr Oberst.'

'Then get through to Snapdragon, tell him to get to Reigate library and find a copy of *Who's Who*. It will tell you everything you need to know about Lord Covington: where he was born, who his parents are, where he went to university, assuming he did of course.'

'No need, Herr Oberst, we have one here. It's dated 1938 but he should still be in it. Should I fetch it?'

'Please, Max.'

Bierhoff returned five minutes later with the bulky volume open at the appropriate page, his right index finger indicating the entry headed 'John Harrison Montague Covington'.

'John Harrison Montague Covington,' Bierhoff recited. 'Educated at Eton and Trinity College Cambridge. Studied archaeology and the classics, is now a world-renowned expert on the Roman occupation of Europe. Does not say what he does now, Herr Oberst. Should I ask Snapdragon to go through a more updated copy?'

Vilma shook his head. 'If he is now employed as part of the British war effort, I'm sure they would leave that bit out. No, tell him to go to Trinity College and do some digging. See to it, would you, Max? And could you bring me the latest aerial recce photos please?'

'They are in that file under the latest communications, Herr Oberst.'

Vilma studied the photos as Bierhoff gathered up all the papers for filing.

'Strange,' said Vilma, stroking his chin.

'Herr Oberst?'

'They seem to be digging a giant hole in a southerly direction – if they go much further, they'll be in the sea.'

'It seems the more we know, the less we know, Herr Oberst. I'll contact Snapdragon right away.'

'Thank you, Max.'

– CHAPTER FOURTEEN –

Saturday, September 2nd, 1944, Abwehr HQ, Berlin, Germany.

Much to Vilma's relief, communications were soon back to normal. He had not been long behind his desk when Bierhoff walked in with several messages.

'Anything from Snapdragon, Max?'

'Indeed there is, Herr Oberst, and if I may say so, sir, the plot thickens.'

'I went to see General Breitner earlier this morning, Max. I thought it was time for the head of the Abwehr to become acquainted with Operation Auger. He is as intrigued as we are. He's asked us to give it top priority and to keep him informed.'

'A wise move, Herr Oberst,' agreed Bierhoff, handing over the slips of paper.

Vilma read each sheet in turn and looked up at Bierhoff.

'So Ledbetter went to Cambridge as well, studied Geology and Geography. And now both work in photo recon interpretation. Makes sense, both are highly intelligent, and both would know what they are looking at. Neither can be called up; one is too old and the other needs a stick to walk. This begs the question… why have these two intellectuals been taken off vital war work to stare into a hole in a field?'

'I suppose it depends on the nature of the hole, Herr Oberst.'

'Good point, Max. Are we expecting anything further from Snapdragon today?'

'Impossible to say, Herr Oberst.'

'Tell all the radio operators anything coming in from Snapdragon is now top priority. Have at least one listening to his frequency at all times. I want to see any message immediately.'

'Very good, Herr Oberst. Should I take these messages and put them in the Operation Auger file, or do you want to take them upstairs?'

'Leave them for now, Max. I'll report to the general at the end of the day. Something else may have come in by then.'

Vilma tapped his desk with the butt end of his pencil. He was more than a little irritated with himself. He was supposed to have one of the sharpest minds in the Abwehr building, but he had no clue as to the purpose of Auger. Was it just the code name for the next Allied invasion that everyone knew was coming? If so, what was the connection between this, two academics, and a new hole in the ground? Were they just a bizarre diversion? Why was Snapdragon so convinced there was a link? And then there was Snapdragon himself. With his intelligence operative's hat on, there was no reason nor evidence to suspect Snapdragon's integrity. Even thinking in chess grandmaster mode, the moves seemed orthodox – perhaps too orthodox. *Well*, he thought, *let's get back to the basics. Examine every detail. Study every move.* He wrote the six words in capital letters on the bottom of his jotter, then hurried to the doorway and yelled down the corridor.

'Max!'

Bierhoff marched in. 'Herr Oberst?'

'Max, we need to get proactive about Operation Auger. I don't want to find out about it all after it's happened. I want you to look into the civilian hole examiners again. Let's see if we can't get some pictures.' Vilma picked up his phone and pressed three buttons. 'I want to see Hauptmann Haller right away.' He replaced the receiver.

'The dirty tricks department, Herr Oberst?'

'They have something I might need, Max.'

The phone rang and Vilma just beat Bierhoff to it.

'Vilma. Good. Thank you. Hauptmann Bierhoff will pick them up now. Max, will you do the honours? Another message from Snapdragon.'

'Right away, Herr Oberst.'

Bierhoff and Haller passed one another in the doorway.

'Come in, Kurt,' Vilma said, beckoning him in.

'Thank you, Herr Oberst. How can our department be of service?'

'Last week a British agent drop went wrong and you're now the proud owners of a Lysander aircraft.'

'Indeed we are, Herr Oberst. The damnedest thing. The pilot decanted his passenger, got caught short, went to do what a bear does in the woods and, lo and behold, a passing patrol came upon it. A pilot armed only with an eight-shot hand gun is no match for a dozen soldiers, so he hightailed it.'

'So where's the aircraft now?'

'Le Touquet airfield, Herr Oberst.'

'Couldn't be better. Has it still got all its RAF insignia?'

'It has, Herr Oberst.'

Bierhoff re-entered the room with the latest post. He placed it in front of Vilma and turned to leave.

'No, stay, Max. I need you.'

'As you wish, Herr Oberst.'

'Have a seat, Kurt. You'll need to take notes. Max?'

Bierhoff sprang to life and placed a pad of paper and a pencil in front of Haller.

'OK, Kurt, your Lysander is going on its first mission. Our photo recon planes run the gauntlet every time they fly over England, but often they have to fly too high and too fast to get good close-ups. Tomorrow morning, at ten hundred hours, it will fly over a hole in a field in Kent. Max will give you the coordinates. Alongside the on-board rigid cameras, I want two hand-held cameras as well, equipped with telescopic lenses. The Lysander can fly very slowly, but we probably will get only one pass. I want as many pictures as possible.'

'What exactly are they taking pictures of, Herr Oberst?'

'This,' answered Vilma. He produced a photo of the excavations from his desk draw. 'It should be full of heavy machinery and people. Cover as wide an area as possible. If all goes to plan, you should be recognised as a friendly aircraft.'

'May I take this photo with me, Herr Oberst?' Haller asked.

'Be my guest,' replied Vilma. 'Could this plane fly straight from Dover to Berlin?'

'It would be close, Herr Oberst, but most of the journey will be over German-held territory. A single

British plane, and a fairly slow one at that, would never make it – no one knows there are Germans in it!'

Cover every move, thought the chess grandmaster.

'Way ahead of you, Kurt. We will send out two 110s to meet it over the Channel and escort it back to Berlin.'

Haller looked doubtful.

'Herr Oberst, if it's to fly across the Channel and back before heading for Berlin, then it won't have enough fuel.'

'Damn,' Vilma cursed, looking frustrated.

'Herr Oberst, may I?' asked Bierhoff.

'Of course, Max.'

'I appreciate that we're trusting to luck on this mission, but may I ask, why ten in the morning?'

Vilma shrugged. 'No real reason, Max. I suppose because we're in a hurry.'

'Well, Herr Oberst, might logic dictate that they'll be on site soon after the digging is finished for the day? You know, to see what the day's excavations have yielded. Say around 1700? It's only ten-thirty hours. It could be done this afternoon. That way, the Lysander could return to Le Touquet, and the films brought here by overnight courier. The photos could be on your desk by nine. Besides which, tomorrow is Sunday and they probably will not be working.'

'Brilliant, Max, brilliant. Is this doable, Kurt?'

'Can't see why not, Herr Oberst. We fly lots of recon sorties out of Le Touquet. There are aerial photographers at the station permanently. They'll be there and back in half an hour.'

'Right, this is the plan. The Lysander will take off at sixteen-fifty hours and fly directly over the site. Lysanders fly back and forth to France all the time, so it shouldn't arouse any suspicions. However, to be safe, tell the pilot not to turn back in full view – that will look odd. Tell him to fly northwest for a few miles. He'll soon be out of sight behind the Southdown hills, then swing east out over the Channel, before heading south and back to Le Touquet. Kurt, advise all AA batteries in the Le Touquet area to under no circumstances fire at it. Arrange for a speedy staff car as the courier, making sure the driver has top priority clearance for the trip. Also, send along a high-ranking officer with him as well. I don't want any hold-ups.'

'I'll get on it immediately, Herr Oberst, and I will keep you updated.'

'Thank you, Kurt. OK, Max, what further gems has Snapdragon unearthed?'

'It's difficult to determine its significance to Auger, Herr Oberst. It just says that Covington spent the whole of August 1939 in the Calais area researching a Roman settlement there.'

'Covington is an expert in Roman history, digging for Roman artefacts is part of his job. What possible connection could that have to a pending invasion now? We weren't even at war in August '39.'

Vilma glanced down at his jotter, examining every detail.

'Max, we are too busy today and tomorrow is Sunday. There'll be no one there, but first thing Monday I want you to get hold of the Paris museum. Find out what you can about this Roman settlement near Calais. Covington will probably have liaised with them during his stay.'

'Very good, Herr Oberst.'

'Are we expecting more from Snapdragon today, Max?'

'Doubtful, Herr Oberst. He says he's returning to

Dover later this morning to follow a lead, and he can only contact us from his home base.'

'In that case, just acknowledge his last message and tell him to report as soon as he has anything. And, Max, don't tell him about this afternoon's little Lysander jaunt.'

Bierhoff made for the door, but halfway there, he executed his trademark half-turn and foot stare.

Vilma smiled. 'What's troubling you now, Max?'

'You are seeing the general this afternoon. Will you tell him that you suspect Snapdragon?'

'Good god no. I've got nothing to tell him, other than a faint feeling in my water that may well turn out to be paranoia. Besides, I know the general trusts him implicitly and knows him personally. As far as I am aware, Snapdragon has only been in Germany once in the last ten years and he stayed with Brietner. They guard his anonymity so well that, when the Führer awarded him the Iron Cross with Oak Leaves and Swords, it was delivered to him in England via courier from the Spanish embassy in London.'

'But the feeling in your water, however faint, still remains, Herr Oberst?'

'How do you feel about going off piste for a while, Max? I want to bait a few traps.'

A feeble smile played on Bierhoff's lips.

'I've always wanted to be a real spy, Herr Oberst.'

'Brietner has all the agent's personnel files in a cabinet in his office. I need to find where he keeps the key. I will go and see him at 1600 hours. I'm told he will be leaving early to attend a meeting in the Reichstag this evening.'

Just before four, Vilma slowly climbed the stairs up to

General Brietner's office, clutching a file. He tapped on the windowless door, which was opened by an adjutant.

'Come in, Vilma. That will be all, Falke.'

The adjutant bowed slightly, clicked his heels and left.

'Thank you, Herr General, the Auger file…' said Vilma, handing it over.

Brietner quickly scanned the messages. He was as bemused as Vilma.

'What do you make of it, Vilma – a red herring?'

'That's the way I am thinking at the moment, Herr General, but to be on the safe side, I've got a captured British Lysander taking some close-up aerials later this afternoon, and Hauptmann Bierhoff is going to do some research into this Roman settlement on Monday.'

'Good work, Vilma. Let me know if the photos and the research turn up anything of interest, will you? If you'll excuse me, I need to get away.'

'Of course, Herr General, but just one more thing. I was thinking of putting another agent on the Auger case, agent code name Popeye, but I have no idea of Popeye's present location.'

Vilma knew perfectly well that Popeye was in Portsmouth.

'Good thinking, Vilma.'

Brietner took a set of keys out of his jacket pocket and unlocked the top left-hand drawer of his Black Forest oak desk. He removed a single key and moved slowly toward a solid steel four-drawer filing cabinet. He inserted the key into the single lock that secured all four drawers, turned it anti-clockwise, and slid open the second drawer down. Brietner thumbed through the files, extracted one and examined it, all the while keeping his back to Vilma.

'Popeye is at this moment in Portsmouth, Vilma. Hauptmann Klein can contact him.'

Brietner closed the drawer and returned the key to his desk drawer.

'Thank you, Herr General. I hope this evening's meeting goes well.'

'So do I, Vilma. So do I.'

Bierhoff returned to Vilma's office just after five.

'The Lysander has taken off on time, Herr Oberst.'

'Thank you, Max. OK, let's go on our first joint secret mission. Nothing very dangerous. All I need you to do is keep a lookout in case anyone comes.'

'I'm prepared to start at the bottom, Herr Oberst,' said Bierhoff, joining in the sarcasm.

The two made their way to Brietner's office. As expected it was locked, but it was of no consequence to Vilma. Every office above the rank of Oberst had, in case of their incumbent's sudden death, a skeleton key that opened every office door in the building. Vilma slipped inside. Unlike the filing cabinet, which was new and had a sophisticated lock, Brietner's desk was over one hundred and fifty years old, and its drawer locks had a simple configuration. Many of the desks on Vilma's floor were of similar age and type to the one in Brietner's office, and Vilma had access to them all. He took out a large bunch of aged keys and tried each one in turn. The fourth attempt was successful, and he opened the drawer. Vilma retrieved the lone filing cabinet key and walked carefully across the room, the floorboards creaking as he did so. *God, I'd never make a burglar*, he thought. Having unlocked the drawer, he noted the files were in neat, alphabetical codename order, and he soon located Snapdragon's.

Wary of being discovered, he quickly viewed the contents, put everything back in its rightful place and made off down the corridor with a much relieved Bierhoff in tow.

Slightly out of breath, Vilma slumped in his chair.

'Anything of interest, Herr Oberst?' Bierhoff enquired.

'As far as I could see, it was mostly a diary of their locations and what particular mission they were on. No details or outcomes, just where and what. But it was not a complete waste of time. For instance, I now know his real name is Otto Foehn, but there is no date or place of birth, no parent details, or where he was educated. But, as if the secret service gods want to prolong my torture, there's one snippet of interest.'

'That adds fuel to the fire, Herr Oberst.'

'He spent two years of the Great War in a prisoner of war camp in Scotland.'

Bierhoff once more wore his baffled expression. Vilma put him out of his misery.

'Crash course on recruiting a double agent, Max. If you're at war with a country, you know you'll need to keep tabs on that country long after the war has finished, therefore you will need double agents, and this is one of the favourite – and easiest – methods of recruitment. During the last war, there was no shortage of dead enemy soldiers available. So what you do is collect identity cards and dog tags and you start making a file on them. You do some research and build up a profile. You are looking for someone preferably who is from a remote village, unmarried, only child with dead or elderly parents, all of which makes him fairly anonymous. You then find one of your own agents who has perfect German, and he adopts his identity. Then the *piece de resistance*: you shove him in a prisoner of war camp and, hey presto, he's an adopted German and, as his colleagues were all blown to bits at the same time he was, no one will know him.'

'Still not conclusive proof, Herr Oberst,' Bierhoff ventured.

'A long way from it,' agreed Vilma.

The phone rang; this time Bierhoff won the race.

'Bierhoff.'

He listened intently for a few seconds.

'That's excellent, thank you, Heidi.'

'Herr Oberst, the Lysander has returned and the film is on its way, just as you ordered.'

'In that case, we've an early start, Max. Let's head for bed.'

– CHAPTER FIFTEEN –

Sunday, September 3rd, 1944, Abwehr HQ, Berlin, Germany.

Vilma and Bierhoff waited like expectant fathers in Vilma's office.

'Did the lab say how many photographs we can expect, Max?'

'Around sixty, I believe, Herr Oberst.'

'In that case, we'd better use the big table in the conference room. Will you sort that out please, Max? Clear the chairs to give us more room, and see we have plenty of magnifying glasses.'

No sooner had Bierhoff set down two large magnifying glasses on the long table than Vilma marched in, closely followed by two clerks, each bearing a tray of photographs. They waited for the clerks to leave and then methodically laid the photographs out in rows.

'The clarity of these pictures is excellent, Herr Oberst.'

'If this war had been fought with cameras, Max, it would have been over years ago. German cameras are far superior to British ones. I'm told they use German cameras in British recon planes.'

'Am I looking for anything in particular, Herr Oberst?'

'You will see lots of workmen. What we're looking for is two people not dressed like workmen.'

They moved up and down the rows of photographs, stopping occasionally for a closer look. The silence was interrupted when Bierhoff yelled, 'Herr Oberst! Take a look at this!'

Vilma hurried down the table and held his magnifying glass over the photograph Bierhoff had indicated. It showed two men, one a few years older than the other. Both wore tweed jackets, shirts and sweaters. One's shirt was open necked, the other wore a tie and both had on stout boots. Vilma couldn't contain his excitement.

'It has to be them!' he exclaimed.

Bierhoff held aloft another photograph, similar to the first but at a slightly wider angle. Both studied it closely.

'Look at this, Max, on the ground by the shorter one's feet. Those are instruments of some sort, not workman's tools.'

Putting the two photos to one side, they carefully went through the remainder, keeping some for the Auger file and discarding the rest. They returned to the two originals and studied them again. A knock at the door caused them to raise their heads. A young female clerk popped her head around the door.

'You asked to be kept up-to-date about messages from Snapdragon, Herr Hauptmann. There is nothing so far.'

'Thank you, Heidi.'

'Strange, don't you think, Max? A top drawer agent witnesses a reconnaissance plane flying very low, and very slow, over an area he's supposed to be observing and he doesn't report it.'

'Decidedly, Herr Oberst.'

'And I'll tell you something else, Max. Frank Ledbetter contracted polio when he was a child and has been a semi-cripple ever since. Neither man in these photos has a walking stick.'

'So they aren't Covington and Ledbetter, Herr Oberst.'

'Snapdragon has gone out of his way to convince us that they are. If he's a double agent, he could have been in Whitehall yesterday rather than Dover. Also, he didn't know about the Lysander. If these are bogus Covington and Ledbetter we may have called his bluff. This means that the real Covington and Ledbetter must be somewhere else – but doing what?'

'Perhaps my call to the Paris museum might shed some light on it, Herr Oberst.'

'No, forget that, Max. I want you to fly to Paris first thing tomorrow and go to the museum yourself. There's probably someone on staff here who knows about history. Find that person and take him with you.'

'I already know that, Herr Oberst. Oberleutnant Shwartz – he's forever quoting historical facts.'

'Good. Tell him to report in tomorrow at 0800 hours. Max, I want you both to glean as much information as you can. Find out what the Romans had near Calais and also about Covington. You may strike lucky and speak to someone who's met him. If you do, without being obvious, get him to describe Covington.'

'I'll do my best, Herr Oberst.'

'Take the rest of the day off, Max. Go home. You deserve it.'

– CHAPTER SIXTEEN –

9am, Monday, September 4th, 1944, Cabinet War Rooms, London, England.

Covington, Ledbetter and Bushell sat nervously on a green leather upholstered bench outside the main conference suite of the Cabinet War Rooms. Abruptly, the double doors opened, decanting an immaculately turned-out corporal who politely asked the trio to follow him. Bushell seemed confident, while Covington and Ledbetter's nervousness was rapidly turning to trepidation.

Churchill sat majestically at the head of the giant table with Eisenhower on his right and Montgomery on his left. The rest of the table was crammed with the highest-ranking officers from all three services, British and American. Churchill bade them welcome and Bushell set down his briefcase, rolled up maps and diagrams at the opposite end of the table. The three seated themselves on the chairs provided.

Churchill aimed the butt end of a giant cigar at Bushell and growled. 'Well, Peter, I have read the abridged version of your Operation Auger. I was expecting something extraordinary and bizarre and by golly, you have not let me down! But in this war, the extraordinary and bizarre has worked well before and I see no reason why it might not work again. I need not remind you, gentlemen, of the dire situation we find ourselves in. All the hard work we have done, the sacrifices that have been made to put ourselves in a strong position, may yet be in vain. Peter, we are relying on you to pull a very large rabbit out of a very large hat – the floor is yours.'

'Thank you, Prime Minister. Before I begin, could I ask someone to contact the Met Office and send over a weather forecast for the next few days for the Dover-Calais area?'

Churchill pressed the intercom button in front of him. Over the crackling, a voice said, 'Yes, sir?'

'Get hold of Stagg at the Met Office. Tell him I want a weather forecast for the Channel area for the next week, as accurate as he can make it. Tell him I want it here in less than half an hour. Carry on, Peter.'

'Thank you, Prime Minister. Can I start by introducing my colleagues? On my right Jack Covington, and on my left Frank Ledbetter. Both are distinguished Cambridge graduates. I haven't time to go through their life histories, but between them they have extensive knowledge of geography, geology, history and archaeology. Since 1939, they've been putting these skills to good use in the Central Interpretation Unit, deciphering aerial photographs – and very good at it they are too. In fact, so good, I had to shift hell and high water to get them, and I've made a solemn promise to have them back by the end of the month.

'Gentlemen, at our last meeting it was agreed that if

progress was to be made out of Normandy, it would necessitate getting the Germans to move masses of their defence armour, thereby giving our troops a much better chance of breaking out. It was further agreed that the only possible way of doing this would be to stage another cross-Channel invasion, this time in the Calais area. The received military wisdom around this table thought it would have precious little chance of success.

'So the only answer is to fool the Germans into thinking the second invasion is coming – and that's where this pair with their particular talents come in, along with myself. And, well, you all know what I do for a living.'

Laughter broke out, which seemed to make the room more receptive. Bushell detected this and decided that this was the moment to strike.

'We intend to let the Germans find out about our little plan. Make them think they've been jolly clever in doing so. They already know some sort of invasion is coming, so the job's half-done. But what they don't know is the form it will take, until we let them know of course. Please remember, the invasion plan I'm going to reveal to you is not going to happen. It's a hoax, so please don't start working out casualty figures!

'Gentleman, the plan consists of three forces: force one takes out the shore batteries from behind, force two is parachuted in and protects force one's back, and force three is the main seaborne invasion force landing on the Calais beaches.'

Bushell deliberately halted his delivery, waiting for the response he knew was coming.

Eisenhower was the first to crack. 'OK, Commander, I'll play the fall guy. How does force one get ashore?'

Bushell let the question hang for a few seconds.

Covington and Ledbetter knew what was coming and both stared at their feet. Bushell dropped the bombshell.

'Through an old Roman tunnel under the Channel.'

The room descended into chaos, a combustible mixture of disbelief, howls of derision, outbursts of laughter and anger in equal measure.

Churchill raised his hands and begged for quiet and a return to some decorum.

'Gentlemen, please, let Peter finish.'

The hubbub quelled and Bushell continued.

'Please remember, what we're trying to do is convince the Germans such a tunnel exists, and its existence is not as outlandish as you think. I will now pass you over to my colleague, Jack Covington.'

Ah well, thought Covington as he rose. *Into the lion's den.*

'Gentlemen, the idea of a tunnel under the Channel is not new. In fact, it's centuries old. The Normans, the Romans and many other French rulers over the years have considered its viability and there is plenty of evidence to support this. The Kaiser in the last war, if his army got to the coast, was planning a feasibility study as a way of invading England. Napoleon even went as far as commissioning plans. As far as we know, no one got as far as putting a spade in the ground, except perhaps, the Romans.'

Covington quickly scanned the room. It seemed the hostility and downright incredulity had been replaced by a polite willingness to listen, even if most of them did think he was barmy.

'In 1939, I was searching an area just outside Calais, prompted by a map from around 50 BC. As you know, gentlemen, time is pressing, so I'm leaving out the details of most of my research and how I found the map, etc. – it's not important. What is important is what's on the map. It is of the wider Calais area, covering an area roughly ten miles by ten miles, and the main features are a massive forest, a small town and a road leading from the town to a small hill with a horseshoe-shaped indentation. We know the forest existed and we know it was all felled over about five years. We also know the town was there. Indeed, small parts of it still exist, as does the road.'

Covington again cast his eyes around the room. The mood had palpably changed again. There was now genuine interest. *Strike while the iron's hot*, he thought.

'Also marked on the map, gentlemen, is the route of a tunnel under the Channel. At the bottom is the signature of Lucius Paulus, so we assume it was he who drew it. Lucius Paulus was a very famous Roman, probably the most pre-eminent architect and designer of the Roman era. Along with some French help, I discovered the site of the town and the road leading from it to the small hill. I was about to conduct some further investigations, but the Germans invaded Poland. Some years later, Frank and I were studying aerial photos of this same area. It was our remit to gather as much information as possible about the French coast, in preparation for D-Day. I'll now let Frank continue the story.'

Ledbetter nervously got to his feet. Covington was used to giving talks, either to students or like-minded groups. Ledbetter had never talked to an audience in his life – and here he was breaking his duck by speaking to a room full of the most powerful men in the world. Moreover, he was trying to convince them that something highly unlikely, even fanciful, might be possible. *Into the breach*, he thought.

'Thank you, Jack. Gentlemen, if I can first expand on our interpretation of the photos? Aerial photography gives us an entirely different perspective of land features – a perspective you could never get from ground level. The location of the town, the road, the small hill and the forest are clearly visible in the photos, but it was the small hill that was of particular interest. Jack has already mentioned the horseshoe-shaped indentation. It's about seven feet high at its highest point and approximately six feet wide and is very symmetrical. I deduced straight away that this feature was man-made, I do not doubt that. We therefore arrived at the theory, albeit very simplistically, that this was the entrance to the tunnel. The trees from the forest were used to shore up the tunnel and the town housed the workforce. Our best guess is it never got much further than the construction of an ornate entrance.'

Ledbetter had never been so glad to sit down.

Bushell seemed pleased with their efforts and he nodded approvingly.

'Thank you, both, I'm sure everyone, while a long way from being convinced, is now a little less hostile to the idea. What I do need to remind you, gentlemen, and at the risk of repeating myself, we are not trying to convince the Germans of the existence of this tunnel. We want them to think we are *sure* it exists. If we can do that, the Germans will be convinced of its existence. Before we move on to the nuts and bolts of the operation, do we have any questions?'

Montgomery raised his arm.

'If the tunnel wasn't actually built, which seems likely, what happened to all that wood from this giant forest?'

Bushell turned to Ledbetter. 'Do you want to take this?'

'The truth is we don't know, General, but it's a fair assumption it went for boat building. The Romans were prolific builders of ships to carry and provide for their vast armies overseas. It's right on the coast and tunnel diggers could very quickly become boat builders.'

Another hand shot up, this time a naval one.

'How far do you think the tunnel got from the French side, and if it was, as you say, more than ten yards, why was the entrance sealed up?'

This time Covington took the question.

'Our best guess is that only a token effort was made at construction. Maybe nothing more than the entrance frame. In which case, it would have grown over again fairly quickly. If they tunnelled a few yards before giving it up as a bad job, they would have restored the land. The Romans were not used to failure and they certainly would not want to leave a monument to one.'

The Q and A was brought to an end by a loud rap at the door, and upon Churchill's command to enter, the corporal took two strides into the room.

'Message from the Met Office, sir.'

'Hand it to Group Captain Henshaw, would you?'

'Sir.'

Like every good military clerk, the corporal made it his job to recognise important visiting officers and made straight for Henshaw and handed him the information.

'Well, Bill,' said Churchill. 'Are the weather gods smiling upon us?'

'It appears so, Prime Minister. There's a large area of high pressure coming in from the Azores. We should have fine, calm weather until at least Saturday. However, a deep low is forming in the Atlantic and it's heading our way. Looks as if it could be the first of the autumn storms, Prime Minister. Should be with us by Sunday.'

'Does this change anything, Peter?' Churchill asked.

'Indeed it does, Prime Minister. I can now be more definitive in my explanation of Operation Auger. So with your permission, sir?'

'The floor is yours, Peter.'

'I'm obliged, Prime Minister. The first thing I need to establish, gentleman, is your state of readiness. Is there any reason that you could not be ready to go in forty-eight hours? General Eisenhower?'

Eisenhower gave a cursory glance around the table. He detected no dissenting faces.

'We have been at readiness level for several days now. Forty-eight hours gives us enough time to come to action stations.'

'In that case, gentlemen, A-Day is Friday the 8th of September and zero hour is 0500, an hour before sunrise. I'll fill you in later on what events need to take place plus or minus zero hours.'

'A-Day?' Churchill questioned. He answered his own question. 'Ah, Auger Day! Carry on, Peter.'

'Gentlemen, Operation Auger has two elements to it – the military side and the deception of the Germans. If I can fill you in on what the Germans know so far in terms of Auger…'

Peter went on to explain the plan, and Covington and Ledbetter's involvement in it.

'Gentlemen, the more observant of you may have noticed that Messrs Covington and Ledbetter are here in this room and not in Kent. That's because we need them here to help carry out Auger and that the two gentlemen purporting to be them are two of our agents. The Germans believe implicitly they are Jack and Frank and have absolutely no idea that they are not. Any burning questions before I move on, or shall we leave it until the conclusion of the briefing?'

The room stayed silent, which Bushell took as the signal to proceed.

'While in the Paris museum in 1939, Jack made the acquaintance of the history curator, one Didier Pascal. On Saturday, he received a visit from two members of the resistance, who are known personally to Pascal. They delivered the map Jack mentioned earlier to him, along with some aerial photos and others taken from ground level from Jack's collection. Pascal was also briefed to expect, sometime over the next couple of days, a visit from some Germans. You see, gentlemen, the Abwehr will now have a team working on Operation Auger and we have more than enough confidence in their skills that one of them will twig that the Paris museum might be a good place to start. It could be as early as today—'

Churchill interrupted. 'This Pascal, is he a member of the resistance?'

'No, Prime Minister, he isn't.'

'And he's simply going to hand over the map and photos, just like that?'

'As you know, Prime Minister, we sometimes have to accept that not everyone is under our control and we have to take calculated risks. We have to rely on people saying and doing what we think they will. In this case, it shouldn't be too difficult as all Pascal has to do is tell the Germans the truth. In fact, he will be encouraged to do so – with one exception. The Germans will be told that the map and photos were posted back to the museum by Jack, as he had to leave Calais in a hurry because of the outbreak of war – all perfectly plausible, the Germans have no reason to assume otherwise.'

Churchill was not totally placated.

'Nevertheless, Peter. This Pascal's nerves will be on edge following the unexpected visit of the resistance. How can you be sure he won't go to pieces when the Germans arrive?'

'We can't, Prime Minister, not one hundred per cent. But in our favour, Pascal knows both resistance members, one he went to school with, and he has been told to pre-empt the Germans with the only small untruth he has to tell. He will introduce into the conversation how the documents got back to the museum before they had a chance to ask. On top of that, with what Jack has told us about him, coupled with our own research, we have compiled a profile of Pascal, albeit a bit of a rushed one, and it suggests he will come through for us.'

For the moment, Churchill seemed satisfied, so Bushell pressed on.

'The resistance has, of course, got the museum under surveillance and will debrief Pascal as soon as the Germans leave. That information will be passed on to us. Gentlemen, this will be the first time in our attempted deception of the Germans that will make mention of the tunnel. Utter disbelief will be the first reaction, as you can imagine, but because of what they already know about Auger, they can't dismiss it out of hand. It's then that we have to give them more and more pieces to enable them to complete the jigsaw.'

Bushell caught Churchill's eye, indicating it was time for a break.

'That concludes the first part of the presentation, gentlemen. I think a break is in order. After which, I will run through the timetable for Auger.'

– CHAPTER SEVENTEEN –

9am, Monday, September 4th, 1944, Paris Museum, France.

Bierhoff and Oberleutnant Schwartz walked through the ornate portal of the Paris museum and entered a typically French, overtly but exquisitely decorated foyer. Sitting behind a heavy, beautifully crafted table was a stern-looking middle-aged lady. The frosty reception did not bother Bierhoff. He'd seen it from French people a thousand times before.

'Good morning, Madame,' he greeted politely. 'Is the curator in?'

'Monsieur Pascal is in his office. Would you like me to summon him?'

'Thank you, Madame, that would be very kind.'

The receptionist picked up the receiver of one of the three phones in front of her.

'Didier, there are two German officers here to see you.'

The two officers pulled a respectful distance away from the table and took in the splendour of the foyer. Pascal appeared from one of the many corridors that met at the foyer. Bierhoff spoke first.

'Good morning, I'm Hauptmann Bierhoff and this is

Oberleutnant Schwartz.' Bierhoff slowly looked around him. 'I must say, no one can beat you French for your stunning architecture.'

Pascal smiled with gratitude.

'Thank you, Herr Oberst. I'm Didier Pascal the museum curator. How can I be of help?'

'We believe you know an English expert on Roman history – a Lord Covington?'

'Yes, I know Jack Covington.'

'How did you meet him?'

'He came here in 1939 with one corner of a two-thousand-year-old map. We searched the section where the rest of the map was most likely to be and, against all odds, we found it.'

'And is the map still here?'

'It is back here now, yes.'

'What do you mean "back" here?'

'Jack took it with him to do his research. He had no time to return it in person when war broke out as he had to return to England in a hurry, so he mailed it from Calais.'

'May we see the map?'

'I'll go and fetch it.'

Pascal returned a few minutes later carrying a long leather tube, a large envelope and some silk gloves. He laid them on the table in front of the two officers.

'I assume you want to look at the map, gentlemen, so if you wouldn't mind wearing these gloves?'

'Of course, the last thing we want to do is spoil it,' Bierhoff assured him.

While the pair donned their white gloves, Pascal carefully extracted the map from its case, and with equal care, laid it on the table.

'What are we looking at here?' Bierhoff asked.

'To the best of our knowledge, Herr Hauptmann, it's an area of about sixty square kilometres in the Calais area.'

'And the signature at the bottom?'

'That is the signature of the famous Roman architect Lucius Paulus.'

'Yes, I think I may have heard of him,' Schwartz lied.

Bierhoff nudged Schwartz playfully on the shoulder.

'The Oberleutnant here fancies himself as a bit of a history buff.'

Bierhoff jabbed a gloved forefinger at the map.

'What are all these other features?'

'That shaded area to the west was a massive forest, felled in the years after this map was drawn. This is the Channel, this is England and this large dot on the coast we think is Calais. And this strange diagram here, Jack thinks is the plans for a tunnel from France to England.'

'What?' exclaimed Schwartz.

'Jack was a long way from being convinced of its existence, but like every good scientist, he was pursuing it until he could prove one hundred per cent its non-existence.'

'And when he returned to England in a hurry, did he go through this tunnel?' asked Bierhoff sarcastically.

Pascal smiled.

'It's not as fanciful as it may sound, Herr Hauptmann. The idea of a tunnel from France to England has been mooted many times over the centuries.'

'Yes, I've read about that,' agreed Schwartz, this time truthfully.

'What's in the envelope?' asked Bierhoff.

'Jack very kindly sent some photographs when he

returned the map,' said Pascal, tipping the contents of the envelope onto the table.

Bierhoff examined the photos, shook his head and asked Pascal, 'Can you decipher any of these?'

Pascal pointed to an aerial picture. 'This mottled area here is where a Roman town once stood. This very faint strip is an old road leading to this small hill, which of course is still there. And this one is a photo of the small hill from ground level. As you can see, it has an unusual feature.'

'Where exactly is this place? Could you point it out on modern-day map?' Bierhoff enquired.

Pascal shook his head.

'There I can't help you. Obviously, as curator, I have a working knowledge of Roman history, but it's not my area of expertise. My passion is France from 1500 onwards. The person you need to speak to is Juste Gilbert. He lives in Calais and knows the Roman history of the area. I recommended him to Jack and they worked together on the site. He worked at the Mairie de Calais before the war.'

'Do you think this Covington is just an eccentric English aristocrat, indulging in some fanciful wild goose chase?' Bierhoff ventured.

'Absolutely not,' said Didier vehemently. 'Jack is a man of integrity and has an uncanny knack for discovery. My hunch would be Jack thought he was onto something.'

Schwartz saw his chance to set the trap.

'I met him once. I travelled to England before the war to hear one of his talks. He is an impressive man and his height gives him an imposing air.'

Pascal took the bait.

'Yes, he is tall and his slim build and shock of hair on top I suppose accentuate his height.'

Bierhoff brought proceedings to a close.

'Thank you for your time, Monsieur Pascal. I'm afraid we are going to have to take these items with us, but don't worry we'll take the greatest care of them.'

As they walked to the waiting staff car outside the museum, Bierhoff smiled and turned to Schwartz.

'You were very good in there. Even I believed you'd met Covington. What made you think he was tall?'

'Well, everything we have learned about him over the last week. I just imagined him in my mind's eye as a tall man. Ludicrous, isn't it, Herr Hauptmann?'

'No more ludicrous than a tunnel under the Channel.'

Before boarding the plane back to Berlin, Bierhoff headed for the adjutant's office. As he entered, the adjutant snapped to attention as Bierhoff handed him a scrap of paper. 'Get me this number please, Adjutant.'

'Of course, Herr Hauptmann.'

A few seconds passed.

'Willy? This is Hauptmann Bierhoff. Inform Oberst Vilma we're about to start back. And priority one, put the feelers out in Calais. I want to track down Juste Gilbert. Works at the Mairie de Calais. Use the Gestapo if you have to.'

With that, the pair boarded the converted Ju 88 for the two-hour return flight back to Berlin.

– CHAPTER EIGHTEEN –

1pm, Monday, September 4ᵗʰ, 1944, Cabinet War Rooms, London, England.

Bushell brought the meeting to order.

'If we may continue, gentlemen. Hope you had a good lunch. I must say, the wartime fare here is a lot better than it is at the Admiralty Building.'

Churchill guffawed, acknowledging the friendly jibe.

'We have only one way of knowing if the deception part of Auger has worked, and that's if the Germans start moving defensive armour from Normandy up towards Calais to meet the invasion. They have sufficient defences around Calais to cope with a regulation invasion, but the threat of thousands of troops pouring out of a tunnel under the cover of darkness and surprising their coastal defences from the rear – well, that's a different kettle of fish. The deception has two elements. Firstly, we have to convince the Germans the tunnel exists, and secondly, make sure the Germans think that we don't know that they know. If both these elements are successful, gentlemen, then the Germans will move the armour and be convinced they are setting a trap for us. They must stay convinced until it is too late.

'And now, gentlemen, on to the timetable. Zero-hour is 0500 hours on the eighth and at zero hour there will be a large explosion somewhere in the vicinity of where the Germans think the tunnel entrance will be, courtesy of our friends in the resistance. The Germans will have been told to watch for such an explosion and that this is the resistance exposing the exit of the tunnel for our troops. A small team of special forces will also be in the area and will set off mortars and fire machine guns, which should lengthen the time before the Germans rumble that Auger is a hoax.

'I'm afraid now is the time for you commanders to start earning your corn. At zero hour, the armada of ships must be in the Channel, about two miles offshore and heading straight for Calais. Likewise, all aircraft. You will all have to do your calculations as to what time before zero-hour ships need to leave their various ports, and aircraft their airfields, to make this happen. Questions?'

'Yes, I have one,' said Admiral Benson, who would oversee the seaborne operation.

'Admiral?'

'When will we know for certain that the Germans have taken the bait?'

'For certain, about 1900 hours on the seventh. That's when we anticipate the Germans will start mobilising their forces north. They will wait for dark, so as not to expose themselves to air attack. We calculate it will take six to seven hours to complete the job and be in position. Of course, we will, through various other sources, have a reasonable inkling before then.'

Benson stared over the top of his glasses at the pad in front of him.

'A quick calculation tells me that the first ships will

have to leave port at around 0400 hours. By which time we will know for sure the bait has been taken and the German defences in Normandy have been considerably reduced.'

'Indeed, Admiral.'

'Have you any insight as to the proportion of the Normandy defences that will be moved to Calais?'

'The short answer is "no", Admiral. However, we are relying, fairly optimistically, on two things. One, they will want to nip Auger in the bud. They must be worried that it will succeed, with the Allies establishing a foothold through the tunnel. Two, the German thirst for glory should not be overlooked. They will see this opportunity for a great victory. Maybe even change the course of the war if they can crush the invasion where it makes landfall. But I repeat, the Germans think we don't know they know about Auger, so they think they have the element of surprise. If things go to plan, we have reasonable confidence the Germans will mobilise a good portion.' Bushell shuffled the notes in front of him. 'After the explosion, when the confusion caused by the resistance and special forces is at its height, we estimate that around 0520 hours phase two will begin. A call sign, known only to a few commanders, will be sent, and all vessels and aircraft will immediately change course to the southwest and head for Normandy. Secrecy is imperative, gentlemen. Very few will know the final destination of the invasion.'

Another uniformed hand was raised. Bushell noted that it belonged to George Leyland, a sharp-as-a-tack colonel in the special forces. The two had worked together before, with Leyland leading several successful clandestine raids. This success was due in no small way to Bushell's intelligence gathering and planning. Leyland trusted Bushell implicitly.

'Yes, George.'

'Just how far are you down the road to convincing the Germans that Auger is for real?'

'The invasion bit is easy. The Germans don't need us to spoon-feed them info on the troop build up. Despite our best efforts, they still have an intelligence-gathering presence over here, albeit on a much-reduced scale, and Berlin is well aware of an impending invasion. They've certainly been intrigued by the excavations and everything else connected. Over the next few days, the pieces will fall into place and the spectre of the tunnel will raise its ugly head. Of course, it will be as outlandish to them as it is to you, but they dare not completely dismiss the possibility. We intend to add several "convincers".

'For instance, on Wednesday morning a flotilla of trucks will deliver to the excavation site a mass of packing crates. With our help, German Intelligence will soon discover the nature of their contents and inform their masters. Which, incidentally, will be thousands of miners' helmets complete with torches and an equal number of oxygen masks and compressed air tanks, just what you need for travelling twenty miles through an underground tunnel. Our double agent will warn them to watch for an explosion exposing the entrance on Friday morning. After that, the Germans, we hope, will be convinced.'

Leyland came back.

'What if between now and Friday the Germans discover the location of this supposed entrance in the photo? Say they excavate it and discover there is no tunnel. They'll know it's a hoax.'

'It would be useful if they didn't find the location,' Bushell accepted, 'but as long as they did so before they had time to examine it more closely, all will be well and good.'

Leyland was not totally satisfied. 'But say they do find it,' he interrupted. 'They will just lie in wait for the resistance to come and lay the charges for the explosion.'

'Not a problem,' Bushell countered. 'The explosion won't be at that location. The charges are already set and will be set off electronically from some distance away. So, if the Germans stake the place outright up until zero-hour, they'll think they're in the wrong place when the explosion goes off. Besides, we are reasonably confident this supposed entrance will not be found. The only reference to it is a two-thousand-year-old, not-very-accurate map. To boot, the only person who could help them, Juste Gilbert, is dead, though the Germans are not aware of that yet.'

Leyland smiled.

'As usual, Commander, you have covered every base!'

Bushell took a sip from the tumbler of water in front of him and proceeded.

'I am not going to pretend this is going to be a cakewalk. The threat of the type 22 U-boats is frighteningly real and they will, of course, be ready for you. Admiral Benson, my department is at your beck and call. We will furnish you with as much intel as we can about the U-boat movements, but, as you know, U-boats are not easy to keep tabs on. Our latest reports do have a modicum of good news, however. A grain ship was sunk in the North Atlantic last night, almost certainly by a type 22. It can't get back by Friday, so that's one we don't have to worry about, and there's a fair chance there would have been a pair of them. Another sustained damage in a recent tangle with a Sunderland flying boat, it is now in for repair. Still, I'm not going to pull the wool, gentlemen, nine type 22s could still wreak havoc with a slow-moving armada.'

Several concerned looks were directed at Benson and he felt he should respond.

'They won't have it all their own way. We will have at least twenty anti-submarine aircraft – Catalinas, Sunderlands and Liberators – quartering the Channel from first light. We also have a new radar. It hasn't been tested in the heat of battle and is so sophisticated that we only have three working units, but the trials have been very exciting. All things being equal, three destroyers should be fitted with them by Friday. It's not going to seriously limit the U-boats' potential to cause carnage, but it should curtail the losses a certain amount.'

'Good to know,' Bushell encouraged. 'One bonus if everything goes to plan: if the Germans are succoured, as soon as they discover Auger is an elaborate hoax, they will be forced to immediately send all their armour back south again. A long line of slow-moving vehicles in broad daylight, unable to fire back. Should be an easy and rewarding target for the RAF.'

'In conclusion, gentlemen, if Auger is successful, then tens of thousands of troops will be landed in liberated France to join the ones already there, ready to advance against a much-weakened enemy. My department will be on twenty-four-hour watch and will leave no stone unturned to ensure its success. However, I'm acutely aware that it's your men that are at the sharp end and I will not hesitate to suggest you abort the operation if I get the slightest inkling something is amiss. Thank you, gentlemen.'

Churchill led the applause. 'Thank you, Peter. Your particular talents, if not assisting us to win the war, have at least kept us entertained. General Eisenhower, can I suggest that this operation is coordinated from your HQ at Camp Griffiss. Second anyone you wish from around this table. I already have a direct line to Camp Griffiss. Peter, can I suggest you establish one too? Right, gentlemen, let's get this show on the road. Or at the very least get packed in readiness.'

– CHAPTER NINETEEN –

1pm, Monday, September 4th, 1944, Abwehr HQ, Berlin, Germany.

Bierhoff, armed with the map and photographs, strode into Vilma's office, excited to share his findings.

'Ah, Max,' greeted Vilma. 'Are we now any the wiser?'

'Indeed we are, Herr Oberst. With your permission, I'd like to start with this photograph the Lysander took of Covington and Ledbetter. Oberleutnant Schwartz took Pascal, the museum curator, into his confidence, saying he'd met Covington. Anyway, we now know he was a tall man, probably around one metre ninety. Our photographic interpreters have scrutinised it very closely and neither of these men in the picture is above one metre sixty-five. You observed, Herr Oberst, that neither man had a stick either. That means it's highly unlikely these two men are Covington and Ledbetter.'

'That's a fair assumption, Max,' Vilma agreed. 'What else have you got there?'

Before Bierhoff could answer, there was a tap on the door and Schwartz's head appeared around it.

'Excuse me, Herr Hauptmann, but a message has just come in from Gestapo HQ. Juste Gilbert was killed in an air raid in 1940.'

'Damn,' he cursed. 'Any further messages from Snapdragon?'

'None today, Herr Hauptmann.'

'Thank you, Uwe.'

'So our top agent has suddenly gone to ground, Max,' mused Vilma. 'What else have you got to show me? And who is Juste Gilbert?'

'If I may show you the map first, Herr Oberst. Covington borrowed this from the museum in 1939. It shows an area near Calais. The museum curator pointed out these areas – a large forest, a small Roman town that's no longer there and a road leading to a small hill with a peculiar indentation. The signature at the bottom is that of Lucius Paulus, a very famous Roman architect.'

Bierhoff indicated each feature as he spoke, but deliberately omitted mentioning the diagram of the tunnel, waiting for Vilma to ask. Vilma obliged.

'And is this just an afterthought, these lines here?'

'No, Herr Oberst. Covington thinks it's a plan for a tunnel to England under the Channel.'

'Good god! You'd better explain, Max.'

'To give you the abridged version, Herr Oberst, the now non-existent town was to house the tunnel workers. The forest provided the means of shoring up the tunnel, and that small hill marks a possible entrance. Covington spent some time at the site just before England declared war and, on the recommendation of the curator, he had assistance from a local expert, the now deceased Monsieur Gilbert.'

Vilma puffed out his cheeks and exhaled

disbelievingly, staring blankly at Bierhoff before uttering slowly, 'Max, please tell me you are not thinking what I'm thinking.'

'I'm very much afraid so, Herr Oberst.'

The two sat in silence for a few seconds before Vilma found the capacity to speak. 'Well, I'm in virgin territory here, Max. This could turn out to be the most elaborate military hoax of all time or the greatest manoeuvre. To me, it's screaming hoax,' he said. '"Examine every detail, study every move",' he recited from his jotter.

'In that case, Herr Oberst, can I suggest we start by thinking that, one hundred per cent, the tunnel does not exist and work from there?'

'Good as anywhere, Max,' Vilma agreed. 'I still think Covington and Ledbetter are the keys to this, so a quick summary of their involvement. They are Cambridge academics and experts in history, geology and geography. When the war started, they went to work in air recon interpretation – nothing sinister thus far.'

'Agreed, Herr Oberst.'

'Now the intrigue begins. Why were they taken off such important war work to go and observe a civil engineering project? Surely two professional surveyors would have been more use?'

'In the practical side of their specialist subjects, the two of them would've had a working knowledge of surveying, Herr Oberst. They could be there as project managers as they are the only ones who know what they are looking for.'

'The entrance to the tunnel on the English side!'

'You observed yourself from the aerials that the workings seem to be pointing towards France.'

'So far, so good. Now it starts to get messy. We know

that two people called Covington and Ledbetter checked into a hotel near Dover. We have established that the two people in the aerial are not them. We have to consider, of course, that the two in the picture may be just two random people. So three questions that we have to answer. One, if the real Covington and Ledbetter are at this site, what are they doing there? Two, if, which seems more likely, the British have planted two substitutes, what is the reason for the switch? Three, if the switch has been made, what are the real Covington and Ledbetter up to now?'

Bierhoff was slowly shuffling the photos, examining each one in turn. He then studied the map, front and back.

'Something worrying you, Max?'

'These ground-level pictures, Herr Oberst. It's logical to assume that Covington took these when he was there in August of '39, and we know he left in a hurry so it's equally logical to think he didn't develop them until he got home. So they couldn't have been posted back to the museum with the map from Calais as the curator said.'

'Well done, Max, and take a look at these aerials. What similarities do you see between them and those from the Lysander?'

'Same size, same clarity, Herr Oberst.'

'Exactly. I'd bet my last two pfennigs that photo was taken with a German camera from a British plane, and a lot more recently than 1939 as well.'

'There is one other thing, Herr Oberst. It may be nothing though.'

'With what we are dealing with here, my dear Max, nothing is going to sound too bizarre.'

'It's just that when the curator brought me the map, I took it out of the tube. The thing is, I was wearing white cotton gloves, and after the map was returned to its pouch, I noticed there was very little dust on the gloves. You'd think that being stuck on a shelf since 1939, you'd expect it to be fairly dusty.'

'It's beginning to look like what we have before us may have been delivered to the museum well after 1939 – maybe within the last week. Max, we have a lot more questions than answers, and we are a long way from establishing a deception. We desperately need more information. Do we have an agent within a hundred kilometres of Dover who we can call upon – other than Snapdragon, of course?'

'Agent code name Everest, Herr Oberst. Based, I believe, just to the north of London.'

Vilma nodded. 'Of course, I've met Everest. Dutch South African, speaks English and Dutch perfectly. Never forgave the British for the Boer War. His parents died in a concentration camp when he was a young child. His cover is that he is a Dutch refugee, being too old to fight, and he works as an animal feed delivery driver. Perfect employment for someone who has to take the odd detour. He's observation only though, I'm afraid. No one questions that he's Dutch, but if anyone with a foreign accent starts asking searching questions, people tend to clam up or even call the police. Max, contact Everest. I want reports from the Dover site twice a day, lunchtime and late afternoon. Likewise, from air reconnaissance. As with the Lysander sortee, have a 110 standing by at Le Touquet to bring the plates straight to us. We'll develop them here.'

'I'll get on it right away, Herr Oberst.'

'And it's time that we brought the general up-to-date as well, Max. We'll meet here first thing and then up to see the general, though I've no idea what to tell him.'

'Very well, Herr Oberst.'

'Just in case, Max, let's keep Snapdragon out of the loop for the time being.'

– CHAPTER TWENTY –

4pm, Monday, September 4th, 1944, the Admiralty Building, London, England.

The war was catching up with Bushell. He was now forty-three and though his ability to deliberate, to process information in milliseconds, to think on his feet, had not diminished an iota, he was beginning to feel his age physically. He had been programmed to think that winning the war came above all else and that casualties were just numbers, not human beings. It was a concept he'd never completely bought into and it was beginning to harm his mental well-being. He cut a weary figure as he trudged into the Admiralty Building. Hustling down the corridor to meet him was Major John Clegg, a senior member of Bushell's inner circle.

'Need to speak to you most urgently, Commander.'

'Problems?'

'Serious ones, sir.'

Bushell gave a resigned sigh. 'Let's head for my office then, John.' Bushell noticed Clegg was extremely agitated. 'You'd better sit down.'

'Thank you, sir. Burdock and Tinwald, the two agents

in Kent pretending to be Covington and Ledbetter, reported in at 1400 hours.'

'And?'

'Well as there was nothing to report, they just routinely touched base. They haven't been in contact since Saturday lunchtime. Then, almost as an afterthought, Burdock mentioned that a PR Lysander flew over the site late on Saturday afternoon. They didn't report it straight away because it flew in from the direction of France, passed directly above them heading northwest.'

'Nothing unusual in that, John. Lysanders do it all the time on one mission or another.'

'Agreed, Commander, but we have been notified this morning that a Lysander on a drop-off mission last week did not return from the operation. Naturally, I checked with all the relevant services and no missions involving Lysanders were flown on Saturday. We also checked with the resistance and they confirmed it is now in German hands.'

'Were Burdock and Tinwald on-site at the time it flew over?'

'Yes, sir,' Clegg confirmed. 'It flew directly over them.'

'Might act in our favour,' Bushell ventured. 'They have no idea what Jack and Frank look like, so it just confirms to the Germans that there are two people who are very likely to be them on site. However, you said problems plural?'

'As per our instructions sir, the resistance kept the museum under surveillance. The Germans were on the museum's doorstep at nine this morning. Two officers, one captain, one first lieutenant. They spent about half an hour in the museum and then left. They went straight to an airfield and took off immediately, one assumes to Berlin. They were almost certainly from the Abwehr, sir.'

'Almost certainly,' Bushell repeated. 'I take it there's more.'

'I'm afraid so. The resistance went to debrief Pascal as soon as the Germans left. It had all gone very much to plan, except for one thing. One of the Germans duped Pascal into describing Jack. They now know what he looks like.'

Bushell spoke Clegg's thoughts.

'So, from the photos they have, they can now deduce that neither of the two men in the photograph is Jack Covington. Still, doesn't really change a lot, does it?'

'Well it might, sir,' Clegg countered. 'The Germans are under the impression that Snapdragon is keeping the site under surveillance when we know he isn't. He's in Surrey. The Abwehr will wonder why he didn't report in about the Lysander, and so begin to suspect his reliability.'

'And I thought this day was going well, John.'

'There's more I'm afraid, sir. Though this time it's only my theory. I think the Germans know more than we are giving them credit for, or at the very least are more on the ball than we thought. They were at the doors of the museum at nine this morning, far earlier than we anticipated. They have probably been over that map and the photos with a fine toothcomb. I rate their operatives highly, sir, and I don't think it will take them long to fathom that the aerial photo of the Calais area is fairly recent, and therefore could not have been mailed from Calais in 1939.'

Bushell visibly sank back in his chair and pondered for a few seconds.

'Let's say you're right, John, and we have to assume that you are. Pascal could be in big trouble. If the Germans pay him another visit and they suspect him of trying to pull the wool, they will not be so friendly this time. We need to act. As a matter of urgency, get hold of the resistance, tell them to find Pascal and get him into hiding, or even better, get him to the Allied-occupied part of France, then we'll know he'll be safe.'

'The museum will be closed now, sir. The resistance will know where Pascal lives, the Germans probably don't.'

'I hope to god you're right, John. It could buy him some time. Contact Snapdragon and tell him not to send any messages to Germany and ignore any incoming ones. He won't know the Germans might be setting a trap. Tell him to get here as soon as humanly possible. He will have to operate from the Admiralty for the time being, at least until this is over. Meanwhile, I will go and see the prime minister and try and explain to him why I misled him and all the Allies leading commanders this afternoon.'

'Beg pardon, sir, I happen to know the PM left for Portsmouth straight after your meeting and won't be back in London until the morning.'

'In that case, John, find out exactly when and notify him I need to see him, priority one. Let me know immediately when you have a time.'

'Very good, sir.'

– CHAPTER TWENTY-ONE –

Early morning, Tuesday, September 5th, 1944, Abwehr HQ, Berlin, Germany.

'Morning, Max,' Vilma said as the Hauptmann walked into his office. 'Any news from Snapdragon?'

'Good morning, Herr Oberst. No, not yet. It is concerning. However, a PR aircraft took off at first light as per your instructions. The photos should be here by early afternoon. By then we should have also received the first report from Everest.'

'Did you sleep well last night, Max?'

It was a loaded question.

'I take it you didn't, Herr Oberst.'

Vilma shook his head.

'After much deliberation, Max, I've decided to delay updating the general, at least until we have more to go on. But first things first. Contact a reliable operative in Paris to immediately go and detain Pascal. If he's not at the museum, then go to his home. If they find him, just detain him, nothing more, until you and Oberleutnant Schwartz can get to Paris to question him.'

'If they find him, Herr Oberst?'

'If I'm right, Max, the resistance will have debriefed Pascal, who will in turn have informed British intelligence. They will now know that Pascal described Covington, put two and two together and realised that Pascal is in peril. Let's hope we are ahead of them. Get Oberleutnant Schwartz to do it right away.'

Bierhoff picked up the receiver of one of the numerous telephones on Vilma's desk and dialled in three numbers.

'Uwe? Priority one, contact Hauptmann Rindt at our Paris HQ. Tell him to get to the Paris museum post haste and detain the head curator, one Didier Pascal. If he's not there, search his home. No, we do not have an address, but someone who works there should know where he lives. I repeat, this is priority one. Time is of the essence. Keep Oberst Vilma's office informed of progress.'

Bierhoff replaced the receiver and turned to see Vilma staring into the middle distance, obviously deep in thought.

'Herr Oberst?' Bierhoff queried. 'You seem troubled?'

Vilma refocused. 'I'm sorry, Max, a mixture of frustration, impotence and ignorance. Auger is driving me up the wall. Even when playing against another grandmaster, I always had an inkling of what he was thinking. The moves he was planning. I feel as if I'm playing blindfolded.'

'A conundrum indeed, Herr Oberst.'

'OK, Max, let us proceed with our proactive strategy. See if we can't solicit a mistake from the British. The fact that we have not heard from Snapdragon only adds further fuel to our suspicions he might be a double agent.'

'I do not follow, Herr Oberst.'

'In this game of intelligence and counterintelligence between us and Whitehall, there are certain unwritten rules, niceties almost, that are observed. Each side gives the other one credit that they are as clever as them, and we do not underestimate one another. Notwithstanding two caveats, which I'll come to later. Snapdragon did not report the Lysander flight because he didn't see it. In other words, he was nowhere near Dover. If British intel is up to snuff, and it will be, they will now be aware that the Lysander is in German hands, and that the flight was carried out at our behest. Similarly, they will know that Snapdragon didn't report it. If he'd been a good little German agent, he would have done. My guess is that Whitehall has forbidden him to have any contact with us, to save him having to answer any awkward questions. He will re-establish contact soon though. Otherwise, it will just confirm our misgivings if the British cut him off altogether. Once the messages commence again, it will just be routine stuff of no consequence. The British are going to have to find another way of drip-feeding us their subterfuge. Pop down the corridor, would you, Max, and tell them just to acknowledge any message from Snapdragon. Perhaps with the odd workaday query, asking to clarify numbers, times, etc. We need to keep the British guessing if we are on to Snapdragon or not.'

'Right away, Herr Oberst.'

Vilma assumed his default position, slumped back in his chair, hands behind his head. Still, his every instinct told him that Auger was an elaborate hoax. But in the chess game that is wartime intelligence, a hoax is played out for a reason, and here Vilma drew a blank. He was wondering if anyone in Whitehall was familiar with the Rubliov gambit when Bierhoff returned.

'Interesting development, Herr Oberst,' enthused Bierhoff, brandishing a piece of paper.

'Enlighten me, Max.'

'It's from one of our friendly observers from the Spanish Embassy who monitors comings and goings into and out of the Cabinet War Rooms. As you can imagine, Herr Oberst, with a possible second invasion on the cards things have been very busy of late, with a regular stream of top brass visiting – no doubt for meetings with Churchill. Well, yesterday morning, in addition to Eisenhower, Montgomery et al, our operative identified three other people who arrived together. One, from the description, we have identified as Commander Peter Bushell, head of Combined Intelligence. The other two are described as a tall man, in his forties with unruly hair, the other a shorter, younger man with a pronounced limp who uses a walking stick.'

'Covington and Ledbetter,' said Vilma.

'Quite so, Herr Oberst,' agreed Bierhoff.

Vilma slowly shook his head. 'Why would Covington and Ledbetter be accompanying the head of Britain's dirty tricks department to go and see Churchill and the Allies' commanders? At least it proves one thing, Covington and Ledbetter can't be in two different places at the same time, so we now know that the Covington and Ledbetter staring into a hole in the ground in Kent are not them – no doubt British agents.'

'Indeed, Herr Oberst,' Bierhoff agreed. 'And as we are sure that Auger is in some way part of the imminent second invasion, it's Covington and Ledbetter's historical expertise they are tapping into, not photo reconnaissance.'

Puzzlement furrowed Vilma's brow. 'Covington and Ledbetter first mooted the possibility of a sub-Channel tunnel, thanks to a two-thousand-year-old map, a forest that is no longer there and a road to nowhere.'

Vilma stopped in his tracks. 'Good god, Max, when I say it like that, it doesn't sound unlikely. It sounds fanciful in the extreme.'

Vilma shook his head as if to reset his brain. 'But all this is on the French side and one assumes that they have, at the very least, a vague idea of where the entrance is. The war will have prevented them from looking for where this fantasy tunnel might pop out of the ground in Kent. So if this fantasy is a reality, surely you would want the two foremost experts in the field at the sharp end directing operations, and not two imposters. Two imposters, I might add, to make us think they are the real Covington and Ledbetter. Meanwhile, the real ones are in Whitehall, working with Bushell and his bunch of con artists on ways to dupe us into thinking there is a tunnel.'

Bierhoff stared at the floor, slowly rubbing his chin.

Vilma smiled. 'Speak, Max,' he encouraged.

'Well, Herr Oberst, let us say for a moment that the tunnel does exist and the British wanted to use it as a part of the second invasion. You can't hide all those earthworks or the arrival of other tunnel-related paraphernalia from our agents or PR aircraft, so what is the first thing you would do if you were British intelligence? Try and convince us it *is* an elaborate hoax so we will ignore it. In the last week, we have discovered who Covington and Ledbetter are and what they do. They made us believe the two people who are observing the excavations in Kent were Covington and Ledbetter. They are even registered in the hotel as such. It screams a hoax. But what if that's what the British want us to believe? What if those two imposters are experts in local history and geology, or able to bring some other relevant expertise to the table? It's our information that Covington and Ledbetter were working at the CIU, but for the last few months, they could have been grubbing about in a Kent field, along with their understudies, coming up with the best-case scenario of where the entrance on the English side could be. For all we know, Herr Oberst, Operation Auger could have begun months ago.'

Vilma once again read out the six words written on his jotter, tapping each word individually with his forefinger as he spoke them.

'Examine every detail. Study every move. Good god, what are we dealing with here, a real hoax or a hoax hoax?'

'And remember, Herr Oberst, your suspicions about Snapdragon now seem justified and it was he who first alerted us to Operation Auger.'

A perplexed hush fell on them both. Vilma broke the silence.

'Have you ever studied science, Max?' he asked.

'Only the normal school variety.'

'When a scientist tries to prove a new theory, what does he do? He tries to disprove it. So let's do that. Let's say the tunnel does exist and the British intend to use it. You went to officer training school, Max, and have seen action, so I'm putting you in charge of the Allied Forces. Using the tunnel as part of your operation, come up with a plan for the second invasion.'

'Could you give me an hour, Herr Oberst?'

'Certainly, Max. We'll meet after lunch.'

– CHAPTER TWENTY-TWO –

Early morning, Tuesday, September 5th, 1944, 10 Downing St, London, England.

The policeman outside number ten offered Bushell a curt salute and accompanied it with a weary smile. *The war is wearing thin on everybody*, thought Bushell as he tapped the imposing jet-black door. A staff member quickly answered his knock, instantly recognised him, waved him in with a respectful nod, and ushered him straight to the Cabinet Room. Churchill, enveloped in the exhaust fumes from a large Havana, bade him sit down on the opposite side of the Cabinet table.

'Good morning, Peter, now what is so urgent that we have to meet at this ungodly hour?' asked the prime minister from amidst the smoke, 'Problems concerning Operation Auger, no doubt?'

'Sod's law with Murphy's variation, plus some unforeseen wartime bad luck to add to the equation,' lamented Bushell.

'That bad, eh?'

'An extremely concerned John Clegg was waiting for

me after yesterday's meeting to fill me in on the day's happenings. None of which was good news. However, Prime Minister, having slept on it, we're still far from being rumbled and the situation is retrievable.'

Churchill took a long, thoughtful drag on his cigar before filling the air with another cloud of blue smoke.

'Fill me in, Peter. Abridged version if you please.'

'Well, sir, our problems began when the Germans captured a Lysander a couple of weeks ago, through the most damnable ill luck. It was a routine drop-off. The pilot went off to spend a penny and a small German patrol that shouldn't have been in the area came across it. Fast forward to last Saturday and the Germans send it over to Kent to get close-ups of the site, where our two agents posing as Covington and Ledbetter were working.'

'You think the Germans managed to snap them, Peter?'

'I believe they even obligingly looked up, Prime Minister. But the problems don't end there, a kind of synchronicity kicked in that even Jung couldn't have forecast. First of all, our two agents did not report the Lysander until 1400 hours yesterday, and only then in passing. Perfectly understandable really, a British plane heading inland wouldn't have raised an eyebrow. But that is not the main problem. We believe the Germans may be onto our main double agent, codename Snapdragon.'

'Basis for those beliefs?' Churchill asked.

'Well, if the Abwehr had no suspicions, they would have pre-warned Snapdragon about the Lysander's visit, which they didn't. Either way, they would have expected him to have seen it and reported it, which of course he couldn't do as he was seventy-odd miles away at the time, and not where the Germans expected him to be, i.e. watching diggers at work in a Kentish field.'

'And have the Germans questioned Snapdragon's negligence?' Churchill asked.

'No, sir, there has been no communication either way in the last thirty-six hours, but we will re-establish contact. Otherwise, the Germans will know for sure if we keep silent. Just run-of-the-mill stuff, messages of no consequence. But it will mean we can't use Snapdragon any longer to feed relevant info to the Germans. They simply won't give it any credence.'

Churchill's concern was growing. 'But did we use Snapdragon to leak the existence of Operation Auger to the Germans in the first instance?'

'We did,' Bushell confirmed, 'but only to sow the seed that there was an operation called Auger in the wind. They have had confirmation of the existence of the operation from various of their own sources. In fact, they would have been more suspicious if Snapdragon had not brought it to their attention.'

Churchill was placated, if only slightly. 'Any more dominoes to fall, Peter?'

'I'm afraid so, Prime Minister,' Bushell conceded. 'The Germans were far more on the ball than we expected. We knew they would join the dots and make the museum connection and head there to question the curator, but we thought this morning at the earliest. Two high-ranking Abwehr officers arrived at 0900 hours.'

'Did the meeting go well?'

'For the most part, Prime Minister.'

'For the most part is not very reassuring, Peter.'

'Two things went amiss, sir. The Germans duped the curator into describing Covington – that would confirm to them that neither of our agents in Kent is Covington. Secondly, the envelope that the curator handed over to the Germans along with an ancient map. It contained some photos – some that Covington himself took, the rest aerials. The Germans might buy that Covington found time to have his photos developed and post them back to Paris, along with the map, before dashing back to Blighty in 1939. But Abwehr officers are not stupid, and in no time at all they would decipher that those aerials are circa 1943. And, Prime Minister, it's my fault. I thought the aerials were pre-war and I should have checked.'

Churchill pointed the butt end of his cigar at Bushell, grave concern etched on his face. 'If the Germans now know the key piece to this jigsaw is the museum curator, and if they get to him, Auger is dead in the water.'

'Well, there I can bring you at least a snippet of glad tidings, Prime Minister. The resistance picked up Didier Pascal in the early hours of this morning and he's now safe behind our lines. At least I managed to get that right.'

Churchill vigorously shook his head. 'Pah! Do not reproach yourself, Peter. Show me a man who can't make mistakes, and I'll show you a man who can't do anything. So where does this leave Auger? I can't see how we can correct this series of faux pas.'

'We don't try, Prime Minister.' The impish but determined smile on Bushell's face captured Churchill's full attention. 'We use it in our favour.'

Churchill guffawed. 'I've seen that look a thousand times before, Peter and it inevitably leads to me having to place my head on the block. But thus far, no one has managed to lop it off. Go on.'

Bushell leaned forward and clasped his hands

together on the table. 'So far, Prime Minister, we've been trying to convince the Germans that the tunnel is real and is part of the impending invasion. The Abwehr, despite being highly sceptical of its existence, are duty-bound to investigate. To date, they've been right on the money with their work, and coupled with our little slip-ups, they are now more convinced it's a hoax. So let them think that. Meanwhile, we change tack slightly. We continue to try and persuade the Germans that the tunnel is real. Indeed, double our efforts on the task. But we adopt a new way of preventing the Germans from finding out about the tunnel. We convince them it's a hoax. It may even be a better plan than the original.'

'It just may be,' mused Churchill, 'it just may be.'

Bushell was now in overdrive. 'It will mean feeding the Germans a constant, heavy dual diet of bogus info, incontrovertible proof that the tunnel exists and will be used, and equally incontrovertible proof that it's a hoax and it's our way of preventing them finding out it's real.'

'So, let me get this right, Peter. We know the tunnel doesn't exist but we want to convince the Germans it does. But we are trying to keep it under wraps, and the way we do that is to persuade them that it's a hoax. In other words, we are trying to sell them a brace of hoaxes alongside each other.'

'Well put, sir, but time is of the essence and we now have to come up with rafts of convincing info and ensure it comes to the attention of the Abwehr. Sir, could we postpone A-Day until Saturday, just to give us more time?'

Churchill nodded, 'Twenty-four hours' delay shouldn't be too much of an inconvenience. I'll inform Eisenhower at once.'

'And I'll contact the resistance to tell them of the delay.'

Churchill squirmed uneasily in his chair, the preamble to a vexed question. 'Peter, quite clearly you cannot use Snapdragon any longer as your purveyor of dodgy messages for German consumption, so what is your alternative?'

'The thing is, Prime Minister, the CIU is neither infallible nor omniscient, and we know that there are still a few German agents out there that have slipped through our net. I'll stake my reputation that there is at least one of them in the Dover area even as we speak. Ah!'

Bushell stopped in his tracks.

'Brain working in a different time zone than your tongue, Peter?'

'Kind of, sir. We don't want to present the Abwehr with Snapdragon's head on a platter, as it were. Our field in Kent will be a hive of activity this week and the Abwehr's new man on the spot will be sending in regular reports detailing them. If Snapdragon doesn't do likewise, they'll know for sure he's a cuckoo. Besides which, I've just thought of an important job for him. No, we'll keep the Germans guessing about Snapdragon for the time being. The resistance is part of this as well, Prime Minister. They are very active in sending radio messages and the Germans have cracked one of their radio codes. The resistance knows this, so it's the one they always use when they want the Germans to find out something. Prime Minister, may I take my leave of you now? I have got a lot to do.'

'Yes, please go,' Churchill snorted good-naturedly, pointing to the door. 'I've had quite enough subterfuge for one morning.'

– CHAPTER TWENTY-THREE –

Mid-morning, Tuesday, September 5th, 1944, Whitehall, London, England.

Bushell quickly gathered together his inner sanctum and briefed them on his meetings with John Clegg the previous afternoon, and the prime minister earlier that morning.

'So you see, gentlemen…' Bushell concluded. 'We are going to have to change tack somewhat.'

Sat in synchronised bewilderment around the table were Covington and Ledbetter, John Clegg, Snapdragon and four other CIU operatives.

'Questions anybody?' asked Bushell.

Ledbetter was first in the queue. 'Just want to clarify, Commander. We are trying to convince the Germans that Auger is both genuine and a hoax?'

'That's about the size of it, Frank. Time is of the essence. Let me go through a 'to-do' list. It may answer some of your questions. We need to busy ourselves with several ruses. This will give the Germans plenty to chew on. Firstly, we need to check that our efforts have not been in vain and our sideshow is dutifully being reported back to the Abwehr. Normally, this would be Snapdragon's department, but our assumption is that the Germans are probably on to him. The Abwehr undoubtedly will already have another agent in Kent. I think it's best we set a little trap.

'Thompson, please call the fire station closest to the site, and ask them to dispatch a fire engine into the field. It just needs to stay there for fifteen minutes, and then turn around and go right back to the station. Stress the urgency.'

Thompson pushed back his chair and made for the door.

'For those of you around this table who are not quite used to our little party tricks...' Bushell shot a quick glance at Covington and Ledbetter. 'We monitor all German radio messages emanating from these shores, both here and in France. If I'm right, a German agent in Kent will report our short, sharp fire engine excursion. He's going to be a busy little spy today because all sorts of things are happening there. I'll come to this shortly.'

Making copious notes and sitting to Covington's left, was a studious-looking young man. *He's barely out of short trousers*, Covington thought. He raised his hand, schoolboy-like. 'Commander, should I alert communications to listen out for any message referring to a fire engine?'

'Yes please, Cartwright, and wherever I am, let me know immediately you get confirmation.'

Bushell's eyes followed Cartwright out of the room. He waited a respectful few seconds after the door closed, and commented, 'If Marconi had not invented wireless, that boy would have.'

'Let's press on, gentlemen,' Bushell encouraged. 'As you now know, A-Day has been moved to give us more time to generously feed the flames of misinformation. At 1045 hours, myself, Jack, Frank, John and you too, Simons, will be leaving for Kent. We will be accompanied by a radio truck. I want you to man this, Simons. Make sure you're in constant touch with our communications room. Get yourself a driver. I'll fill you all in on the way on the purpose of our visit. Cartwright and Snapdragon will be stationed in the communications room. You too, Thompson. You're our procurement man and I may need various materials at short notice.'

'Very good, Commander.'

Snapdragon politely raised his pencil. Before he could speak, Bushell beat him to the draw.

'Yes, we have to be ultra-careful from here on in. You should remain in contact with the Abwehr. Otherwise, it will just confirm their suspicions. For the time being, make like a parrot and just repeat what our unknown agent sends – once he starts, of course. Send one message right away, reporting the arrival of a fleet of lorries at the site. They arrived earlier today, so you will not be lying. If they ask any difficult questions, just stall or give vague answers. We need for you to keep up the pretence and retain a modicum of trust between you and the Abwehr because I will have one last, special job for you.'

Snapdragon raised his eyebrows to encourage Bushell to elucidate. Bushell obliged.

'At a specified time, in the early hours of next Saturday morning, you will send an urgent message to the Abwehr. It will read thus: 'Urgent, priority one, Auger is a hoax. Repeat, Auger is a hoax.' Between now and then, we will undermine your credibility just enough to make the Abwehr further question your loyalties. Therefore, when they do receive this message, they will think you are trying to con them, and word will spread like wildfire that Auger is for real. Gentlemen, to Kent.'

CHAPTER TWENTY-FOUR

Early afternoon, Tuesday, September 5th,1944, Abwehr HQ, Berlin, Germany.

Bierhoff walked into Vilma's office bearing sheets of notepaper in each hand.

'Good news, Max?' Vilma asked optimistically.

'We don't have that kind of luck, Herr Oberst. One bad, two interesting.'

'Let's have the bad one first then,' Vilma decided.

'Pascal, the museum curator, was neither at the museum nor his home, Herr Oberst. His neighbour saw him come home around six and thought he heard a door close around 2am.'

'Probably a futile exercise, Max, but alert all checkpoints, stations, etc. to watch out for Pascal.'

'Already done, Herr Oberst.'

Vilma nodded his approval. 'So, Max, let's move on to "interesting" shall we?'

'Everest has been in contact, Herr Oberst. He reports an armada of trucks arriving at the site.'

'And what bounty were these trucks bearing?'

'Mostly railway sleepers, Herr Oberst, but a couple

of other interesting bits of cargo too. Firstly, what appears to be two very large air compressors and about twenty packing cases about two metres by half a metre by half a metre. Contents unknown. Also, some smaller cases full of hand tools: shovels, picks and what have you. Two smaller diggers arrived just after the trucks.'

Bierhoff paused and stared curiously at the notepaper.

'It also says that a fire engine arrived at the field, turned around and left.'

'Everest has been busy,' reasoned Vilma.

'Not only Everest, Herr Oberst. Snapdragon has also reported this morning's deliveries, though not in as much detail. He also logged the fire engine visit.'

Vilma sat to attention.

'Did Snapdragon report before or after Everest?'

'Just let me check the timing log, Herr Oberst. The truck arrivals before, the fire engine after. He didn't mention the two diggers at all.'

'We are still none the wiser, Max. All this hardware arriving could either be a hoax or reality. Right, Max. You are hereby promoted to Feldmarschall. Tell me your plans for the second invasion.'

'What I've done, Herr Oberst, is set up a sort of war game. Let's start by matching the opposing forces. The area around Calais is heavily fortified with heavy and medium artillery, far more concentrated than at Normandy when the Allies invaded. The sea below the low water mark is well-mined and we, of course, have the new type-22 U-boats. Most importantly, there would be no element of surprise.'

'And the opposition, Max?'

'Well, despite what it may seem like, the Allies do not have an inexhaustible supply of men. The Americans are suffering heavy losses island hopping in the Far East. The Allies are bogged down in Italy and a large chunk of the Allied Forces in Europe are twiddling their thumbs in Normandy. Having said that, Herr Oberst, the invasion force will still be formidable. Our best estimate is about half that which landed on D-Day.'

'And now the big question, Max, will the invasion force be repelled?'

Bierhoff deliberated for a few seconds.

'I think it would, Herr Oberst. The type 22s would make significant inroads before the force got anywhere close to the landing area, and then the mines would account for a small percentage. If the shore batteries are on their game, picking off slow-moving landing craft should be like shooting fish in a barrel. The area is well covered with anti-aircraft guns, so damage from the inevitable pre-invasion air raids should be minimal.'

'Well done, Max,' Vilma congratulated. 'What's more, the Allies must agree with you. Otherwise they'd have come by now. So, what part, if any, could a tunnel play, and would it change the outcome?'

'Almost certainly,' Bierhoff answered, 'because then our strengths become our weaknesses. If you are tunnelling under something rather than through it, you have to dig down first, so any entrance would be some distance from the shoreline, but probably no more than a couple of kilometres. Let us imagine a tunnel two metres square. A whole division could pour through that entrance in not much more than an hour and be heading for Calais before they're even detected. All our artillery pieces point out to sea and the troops manning them would either have to keep firing on the invasion force or defend their positions. They couldn't do both. Either way, they would be fairly quickly overrun. I would also mobilise the local resistance to cause as much havoc as possible between the tunnel entrance and further inland, just to slow up any reinforcements that we may send.'

'From great victory to humiliating defeat, just like that,' Vilma mused. 'Let's not get carried away here, Max. The likelihood of this tunnel existing is still negligible at best. So why are the Allies doing their damnedest to convince us it is there?'

'To force our hand, Herr Oberst?' Bierhoff ventured.

'Of course,' Vilma agreed. He drummed the fingers of one hand on his desk while fingering his tie with the other.

'Max,' he said slowly.

'Herr Oberst?'

'Your second scenario, the one where you have Allied soldiers pouring out of the tunnel like lemmings over a cliff. What would turn that result on its head?'

Bierhoff mulled the question for a few seconds, then clicked his fingers and half-yelled. 'If we knew they were coming! If we saturated the area with troops and artillery, we wouldn't need to know where the tunnel entrance was – it would soon become obvious. The Allies would be slaughtered.'

'But to achieve that result,' Vilma cautioned. 'We would have to move men and materiel to meet the threat, both from the invasion fleet and the mole brigade. And that is exactly what the Allies want us to do.'

Silent contemplation followed, before Vilma spoke again. 'Your military assessment is spot on, Max, and it's led me to a conclusion. The Allies have no intention of launching a second invasion because, as you pointed out, they'd be defeated. So they latch onto some cock-eyed tale about a deranged Roman emperor who fancied invading England without getting his feet wet by tunnelling under the sea.'

Bierhoff frowned, his eyes slightly raised. Vilma watched him, smiled, slowly shook his head, and said, 'OK, Max, out with it.'

'Sensible logic tells me you're absolutely right, Herr Oberst. But the Allies are going to an awful lot of trouble to convince us there is a tunnel and, in some ways, that there isn't. If I can use your science analogy, why not assume there *is* a tunnel? It should be a lot easier to prove there isn't one rather than there is.'

'Good point, and I have another problem. I have a feeling in my water that we're only a matter of days from this volcano erupting. We've no military power; we can't give orders, which means I can't delay much longer taking all this to Brietner. And then he'll have to inform High Command.'

The nearest telephone to Bierhoff rang and he picked up the receiver and with a curt 'right', then returned it to its cradle.

'Another raft of messages, Herr Oberst.'

'Go and get them, Max, and I'll get us a cup of coffee. We'll read them, act upon them and I'll explain the two caveats I mentioned. Hopefully, between then and now, I'll come up with how and what I'm going to tell the General.'

– CHAPTER TWENTY-FIVE –

Late morning, Tuesday, September 5th, 1944. The A2 London/Dover Road.

A military staff car, accompanied by army outriders, sped along the A2 towards Dover. Two seats up front, two bench seats facing each other in the back, and a sliding glass division separating the front from the rear. In time-honoured fashion, the driver sat alone with the glass firmly shut and the four passengers in the back. Rank dictated that Bushell and Clegg faced forwards, which left Covington and Ledbetter staring out the rear window. A Humber radio van followed behind. Simons occupied the passenger's seat while an ATS girl drove.

'This field was not chosen at random,' Bushell explained. 'This one fits our purpose to a tee. Far enough from the coast so that a gentle upslope would have the tunnel emerge without the Channel filling it with water, but close enough to avoid any unnecessary digging. We should be there in about fifteen minutes. I will then bring you up to speed about the next phase. This will be civil engineering at breakneck speed. As far as the wider plans for Auger and A-Day are concerned, things are progressing nicely. More troops have been moved to the vicinity of the tunnel entrance and…'

Ledbetter choked back a laugh. Bushell indulged him, 'Yes, I know, Frank. I speak as if the whole thing is real, but that's the mindset we have to adopt. If we don't believe it, how can we expect the Germans to?'

'Good point,' Ledbetter conceded. 'Would I be right in thinking that these troops will at the last minute head for Dover to board a ship and take part in a real invasion, rather than an imagined one?'

'That's the plan,' Bushell confirmed. 'In fact, the majority of their equipment is already on board, and the field is only a mile and a half from the port. They can march there in about twenty minutes. And the fact they have no equipment at the site is part of the charade. Both sides concede that if the tunnel does exist, it is going to be far from cavernous. Suitable for troops on foot only. Our chaps going through it would carry a rifle or light machine gun, a few grenades and as much ammo as they could secrete about their person, and that's it. Ah! We're here.'

The site occupied several fields, most of which was an army camp. They drove through dozens of symmetrical rows of olive-green tents. Hundreds of troops milled about, blissfully ignorant about the part they would play in Operation Auger, both real and imagined. The car drove through a final gateway onto what appeared to be a building site. On one side was a large mound of discarded soil, and on the other machinery, equipment and materials.

The car drew up at the far end of the field. Covington and Ledbetter were taken aback by the scale of the operation. They had half-expected to see a dozen or so blokes with shovels and picks. They had not anticipated an impressive mechanical excavator dutifully digging out barrow loads of earth in one fell swoop. The wireless truck came to a halt alongside, with Simons already knob-twiddling in the back.

'Just some parish notices before we alight,' said Bushell. 'Many thousands of troops are boarding transport ships in readiness for A-Day. For the Germans to believe that we're heading for Calais, they would expect a heavy bombing raid the night before. Ordinarily, we would oblige them with this, but we're going to employ a double bluff. We will leak the exact date of A-Day to the Germans, so they think that this is no ordinary seaborne invasion. Our friends in the resistance have begun to mobilise, and wireless traffic between their units is getting heavier.' Bushell paused. 'I do wish their radio security protocols were better though.' But his words were not accompanied by a worried countenance. He actually said them rather gleefully.

The staff car decanted its four passengers. No sooner had they alighted than Simons was making for them at a fast walk. He would have liked to yell out, 'They've bought it!' but CIU training had taught him to curb such indiscreet displays of frivolity.

'Messages from Cartwright, Commander. About twenty minutes ago he picked up a signal heading for the Abwehr reporting the visit of the fire engine. It also mentioned delivery trucks and described some of the cargo. Snapdragon sent two separate messages, one about the fire engine, and the other reporting the trucks, but he gave no content description.'

'Did anyone answer Snapdragon's messages?'

'Only acknowledged their receipt, sir.'

There was no hint of 'I told you so' in Bushell's voice as he spoke, no gloating. 'Well, it appears we are being watched, gentlemen. Good. This new chap seems to be on the ball. I think he deserves a title. The first ever cricket match was played not far from here, so let's christen him "Wisden". Ah! Here they are.'

Two men in good quality working clothes approached. Bushell was obviously expecting them. He quickly scanned the site and turned to Simons.

'Get hold of Thompson and tell him to get some more workmen down here. Ask them to report to the foreman when they arrive. A dozen should be enough. Make sure you tell everyone about the codename.'

As Simons took his leave, the two strangers reached the group and Bushell took great delight in introducing them.

'Jack and Frank, meet Jack and Frank! Better known to us as Burdock and Tynwald.'

'Which one is which?' asked Ledbetter, smiling.

'I'm the Manx parliament, he's the weed,' replied the stockier one affably.

Bushell indicated with an outstretched arm that they should move in the direction of where the digger was at work.

'The first thing I need to do is introduce you to the site foreman, our project manager if you like.'

As they approached the toiling piece of machinery, it became clear what the fruits of its labour had achieved. Over a width of about twelve yards, it had excavated a gently sloping wedge into the ground. This was now about thirty yards long, thus creating at the thick end a sheer wall of earth about eight feet high. Their arrival prompted the driver to down tools. He clambered down from the cab, dextrously rolled a cigarette and lit it. From behind the machine appeared a tall, athletic man in working men's garb, carrying a theodolite. As he passed the driver, he used the instrument to point to the canteen van.

'OK, Harry, go and get your dinner.'

The man walked over to Bushell and extended his hand. Bushell shook it firmly and turned to the group.

'Gentlemen, may I introduce Wally the foreman.'

Bushell gave a quick cursory glance around and, satisfied the driver and anyone else was out of earshot, spoke in a lower tone.

'Better known in military circles as First Lieutenant Andrew Harvey of the Royal Engineers. We're borrowing him for a while. For the next couple of hours, I want us to put on an act worthy of the Royal Shakespeare Company. It's unlikely that Wisden is keeping a twenty-four watch on us, but better safe than sorry. I suggest we walk over to that earth wall, and make out that we're planning a serious bit of civil engineering. I guess, to a certain extent, we will be. Wally, you, Tynwald and Burdock must keep up the pretence for the next few days.'

They reached the far end of the excavation and Bushell patted the earth wall approvingly.

'This is perfect,' he enthused. 'Wally, is it possible to dig out a shaft and shore it up with sleepers? About six feet high and three wide. You don't have to go in too far. About fifteen yards should be enough.'

'Perfectly doable,' Wally confirmed.

'Right, gentlemen, let's go and put on a show.'

For the next hour, the group put on a passable impression of a competent bunch of civil engineers. They toured the site, inspecting equipment, waving their arms, pointing and taking notes. Wally even took a couple of readings of nothing in particular with his theodolite. Ledbetter was idly flicking some switches on one of the giant air compressors when he noticed a soldier making his way toward them.

'Army officer at ten o'clock, Commander,' Ledbetter announced.

'Ah! Saves me going to find him,' said Bushell. 'Wally, we don't know who might be watching, so if he salutes, for God's sake don't return it. You are a foreman, not a first lieutenant.'

The officer did salute and Bushell shook his hand.

'Gentlemen, this is Major Gerald Harding and all those soldiers you see over there are his charges. The major is fully cognisant of Operation Auger. As you can see, Gerald, work is progressing. The practical side of Auger is on schedule, and after today's little charade, we hope the chicanery part is up to speed as well. Gerald, in the next couple of days there will be a consignment of miners' helmets arriving, complete with lamps. So too will some, erm, I don't know what to call them, I haven't been given a name. I described what I wanted to the boffins, namely something that looks like a personal breathing apparatus. Apparently they've come up trumps, but I haven't seen the finished article. It only needs to be something that convinces our German guest from a distance. Have your men come in groups to try them on? By the way, as we didn't want to bring the coal industry grinding to a halt by filching several thousand miners' helmets, most of the crates will be empty. Same with the breathing apparatus. We want to give the impression we have thousands of them. The drivers will let you know which ones to open. We will, of course, keep you up-to-date with developments. And that, gentlemen, concludes our business here for today.'

Harding saluted, turned on his heel and made for the camp. Wally, Tynwald and Burdock returned to the main site, while the remaining quartet headed for the staff car. Simons was waiting for them.

'Any messages, Simons?' Bushell enquired.

'The resistance have started to pass questionable radio messages and the PM would like to see you first thing in the morning, Commander.'

'Right-ho, contact HQ. Give a very brief description of our visit and ask Snapdragon to send it in about twenty minutes. Oh, and tell them we are on our way back would you?'

While Bushell and Simons were de-briefing, Covington walked over to the spoil heap where he'd spotted something earlier. He extracted a heavily rusted shaft of metal. He dusted off some of the dirt as he returned to the car. Bushell spotted him.

'You can take the man out of the museum, but you can't take the archaeologist out of the man!' he paraphrased. 'What have you got there?'

'Pretty sure it's an Iron Age tool of some sort, Commander.'

The four reclaimed their seats in the staff car and with the radio truck in tow, they headed back along the A2.

After another debrief in Bushell's office, Covington and Ledbetter wearily trudged their way back to their hotel.

'Drink?' asked Ledbetter.

'Thought you'd never ask,' Covington replied. 'Hotel bar?'

'Fine. By the way, your Iron Age artefact. We both know it's not.'

'No.'

'Is it what I think it is?'

'Almost certainly.'

'A Roman gladius?'

'Hmmm.'

– CHAPTER TWENTY-SIX –

Mid-afternoon, Tuesday, September 5th, 1944, Abwehr HQ, Berlin, Germany.

Vilma returned to his office, a steaming cup of coffee in each hand. Bierhoff was waiting for him. Vilma shuffled through the pile of documents on his desk, drew out a large brown envelope and emptied the contents.

'Could I help in your search, Herr Oberst?' Bierhoff asked.

'Thank you, Max. I'm looking for the photographs Covington took near Calais in 1939. Ah! Here they are. It's a long shot, Max, but I think it's worth pursuing. Get copies of these over to Calais, would you? I want them there by first thing tomorrow. In the meantime, ask our Calais operatives to look up any people who may have local historical and geographical knowledge – teachers, historical societies, local museums, that sort of thing. When the photos arrive, tell them to visit these people and see if they recognise where this hump with a road leading to it might be. Covington obviously thought it was important.'

'The entrance to the tunnel, Herr Oberst?'

'I did say it was a long shot.' Vilma shrugged. 'But if we do get lucky and manage to pinpoint it, we may have time to dig it out. If we find nothing, it'll be another box ticked toward proving it's a hoax.'

'Alternatively, we will find the place where Allied troops will emerge and be ready for them,' Bierhoff reasoned, indicating the six-word legend written on Vilma's jotter.

'Quite so, Max. Anyway, get Shwartz on to it straight away, will you? I can't keep the general in blissful ignorance any longer. I'll schedule an appointment to see him later today.'

'Excellent, Herr Oberst, but there are some important messages?'

'Next thing on the agenda, Max.'

Bierhoff seemed placated and left. Vilma apprehensively reached for one of the phones and slowly lifted the receiver to his ear.

'General Brietner's office please.'

Vilma leaned back in his chair, waiting for the reply.

'Hello, Oberst Vilma here. Would it be convenient to see the general later this afternoon? 1700? Fine. Thank you.'

Bierhoff returned and shuffled the note papers he'd left on Vilma's desk.

'Right, Max. From the top.'

'Well, Herr Oberst, we're picking up increased inter-unit radio traffic from the resistance. There is a continuing reference to this coming Saturday, the ninth as being A-Day – could the "A" stand for Auger?'

'Quite plausibly. So, Max. What else?'

'They seem to be mustering units in the wider Calais area, Herr Oberst.'

'Do you think they are there to back up the invasion or are they helping to embellish the hoax?' Vilma asked rhetorically. 'Go on, Max.'

'The field in Kent had some very interesting visitors this morning. Two vehicles, a staff car and a radio truck. Four men in the car. Everest gave brief descriptions, and it seems it was Commander Bushell and Major Clegg from British Central Intelligence. The other two were possibly Covington and Ledbetter. They met up with two other men who were already there – possibly Covington and Ledbetter's stand-ins?'

'That would have been a surreal moment,' Vilma observed. 'Covington and Ledbetter being introduced to themselves!'

'Not an everyday occurrence, Herr Oberst. They were joined by one of the site workmen and for the next hour they toured the site, inspecting equipment and material. Just before they returned to their cars, an officer from the army camp came over, had a brief conversation and left.'

'Did we hear something similar from Snapdragon?' Vilma asked.

'Almost simultaneously,' Bierhoff answered, his voice laden with suspicion. 'His message was very brief, containing no description. Herr Oberst, Snapdragon should have recognised all four men on sight.'

'Sounds as if he's just going through the motions, Max.'

'The British seem to be going the extra mile to convince us that the tunnel is for real, Herr Oberst, and that overt demonstration was part of it. They will know we have eyes on the site, but if we didn't know what we know, we'd be scratching our heads as to what's exactly going on. To be honest, the idea of a sub-Channel tunnel wouldn't have entered our heads. Its absurdity is its own security blanket. But they know we know about Auger – yet still, they tease us with the hoax possibility. Herr Oberst, we have to discover if the hoax diet we are being fed is a recent change of plan. In other words, they've made a hash of the information we've been fed.'

'I think you are on to something here, Max,' Vilma enthused. 'I'm convinced the original plan was to persuade us of the existence of the tunnel. Hoax was nowhere on their agenda. Auger's sole purpose is to make us move troops and guns to where the invasion isn't going to happen. But having discovered their foul-ups, they are now firing two barrels at us. One, re-doubling their efforts to convince us of the tunnel's existence and two, trying to convince us that it's a hoax to put us off the scent that the tunnel is actually for real! You have to hand it to the British, this is taking thinking on your feet to another level.'

'Do I take it, Herr Oberst, that we are now both happy that it's a one hundred per cent hoax?'

'Ninety-nine point nine per cent, Max. One hundred per cent if we knew for certain the tunnel did not exist. I'm still sticking with the proactive theme. Let's get some help. What we need is an expert in engineering history. Any thoughts, Max?'

'Well as we know, Herr Oberst, we've already made use of Oberleutnant Schwartz's historical knowledge. But history is his hobby, not his profession. Before he joined us, he had just completed his degree in engineering at Heidelberg. Would he do, Herr Oberst?'

'At this late stage, Max, he'll more than do! Get him in here!'

Bierhoff immediately lifted a telephone receiver.

'This is Hauptmann Bierhoff. Send Oberleutnant Schwartz to Oberst Vilma's office would you?'

Within seconds, footsteps were heard in the corridor. There was a polite tap on the door and Schwartz entered.

'Herr Oberst, Herr Hauptmann,' he greeted courteously.

'I'll come straight to the point, Uwe,' said Vilma candidly. 'How outrageous is this idea that the Romans could dig a tunnel under the English Channel?'

Schwartz was in his element. 'Well, Herr Oberst, the things we have to consider are these: the enormity of the task, level of skill needed, available labour, available materials and level of equipment. Let's leave item one for now. The skill level is not high – a few people with a basic knowledge of surveying and lots of people with shovels are about it. Labour, no problem. The Romans were well versed in "persuading" local inhabitants to work for them. About the only material you'd need would be roof props, and the countryside was covered with trees, so not an issue. Equipment, all manually operated, of course, just hand tools. They could do the job, but painfully slowly. Now the big one – the size of the job. I don't know how far men could dig in a confined space, using hand tools, but I think it safe to say, the tunnel would take decades to complete. You'd also have to rig up some sort of ventilation system as you went. And I haven't even mentioned disposing of millions of tonnes of spoil.'

'So what you are saying is the whole thing is totally impossible, Uwe?' Bierhoff prompted.

'Not totally, Herr Hauptmann, virtually. Remember this, two and a half thousand years before Julius Caesar, the Egyptians moved six million tonnes of stone to build a pyramid nearly one hundred and fifty metres high and almost a kilometre around the base. Around the same time, ancient Britons transported dozens of stone columns, weighing more than twenty-five tonnes, two hundred and fifty kilometres to build Stonehenge. And that was after quarrying and fashioning them with virtually stone-age tools.'

'Well thanks for nothing, Uwe!' exclaimed Vilma good-naturedly. 'You've told us exactly what we didn't want to hear!'

'Glad to be of help, Herr Oberst. Will that be all?'

'Yes, thank you, Uwe.'

'We seem to be taking one step forward and two back, Herr Oberst,' Bierhoff said with a sigh.

'Not quite, Max. Remember, what Uwe said didn't increase in any way the likelihood of the tunnel existing. It just didn't rule it out completely. Right, enough for now. Let's us put our heads together and come up with a potted version of what we know about Operation Auger that I can present to the general.'

'Do you want me to accompany you, Herr Oberst?'

'No, Max, no point in the general thinking we have both taken leave of our senses.'

The pair spent the next hour trying to formulate a report that was succinct, believable and that hadn't been written by the Brothers Grimm. Vilma ordered more coffee, took out a cigarette and proffered the pack to Bierhoff.

'I notice,' said Bierhoff, resting his cigarette on the edge of the ashtray, 'that you didn't mention Snapdragon, Herr Oberst.'

'No, but I'm going to have to moot the possibility, Max. I'll just say that the timing and content of some of his messages recently have given us cause for concern, and will quickly counter it by saying that Everest is doing an excellent job and his loyalties are beyond reproach.'

Bierhoff nervously fiddled with his cigarette and Vilma spotted it.

'You have concerns about my meeting with the general, Max?'

'The two caveats you mentioned earlier. Is one of those caveats General Brietner?'

'Yes and no. If you recall, I was talking about the "game" that is intelligence and counterintelligence. The Abwehr and Whitehall are pretty evenly matched, except for the two aforementioned caveats. The average British operative has a slight advantage over his German counterpart in that his thought processes are not quite as rigid. The British guy is more willing to think laterally, outside the box and is not afraid of trying the bizarre. Auger proves this only too well. It's all to do with recruitment. In Britain, it's the politicians and civil servants that appoint the top people in the intelligence services, and although the vast majority do come from the armed forces and have the necessary intellect, they are not afraid of adding a bit of maverick into the mix. Over here, being an army officer of above-average intelligence is very often good enough. We do have a lot of good men here, but we lack that extra factor that would make us better.'

'After dealing with Auger for the last week or so, I can see that, Herr Oberst.'

'Good example indeed, Max,' Vilma agreed. 'But it's the brass at the top of our organisation that are an issue as well. Many are army generals who have been appointed for that reason alone. Most have never worked in the field. Their mindset is in mono-vision. No flexibility, no guile or subtlety. Triumph for themselves and the Fatherland overrides all else.'

'Are you saying that General Brietner is cut from this particular cloth, Herr Oberst?'

'I'm very much afraid so, Max. If we knew the location of Covington's mound at Calais, his solution would be to head straight there with a brigade of Panzers and flatten it.'

Vilma looked at his watch. It read 1750 hours.

'Ah well, Max. Into the lion's den.'

– CHAPTER TWENTY-SEVEN –

Late afternoon, Tuesday, September 5th, 1944, Abwehr HQ, Berlin, Germany.

Vilma sat in silence opposite General Brietner and squirmed uncomfortably in his chair. Brietner looked up from the Operation Auger report and placed it with great care on the desk in front of him. He looked Vilma coldly in the eye and spoke with gravity.

'You realise, Vilma, that I am going to have to take this up to High Command?'

'Of course, Herr General.'

'I really don't know what they will make of it. Hauptmann Bierhoff's assessment of the outcome of the invasion, both with and without the tunnel, is both accurate and commendable. Pass on my compliments, would you?'

'Indeed I will, Herr General. Hauptmann Bierhoff is a very fine officer.'

Brietner laid both palms on top of the report and again stared at Vilma.

'So, Vilma, in your opinion, this tunnel does not exist?'

'Virtually all the data we have gathered certainly points to that conclusion, Herr General.'

'I'm not sure I agree.'

Vilma's heart sank. His worst fears were beginning to manifest themselves.

'May I ask why you disagree, Herr General?'

'On the balance of probabilities, you are more than likely right, the tunnel does not exist. But I do think you are being a bit cavalier in dismissing its existence. Remember, if we don't give it a certain amount of credence and Bierhoff's second scenario occurs, we will lose the war, and very quickly. You haven't explained to my satisfaction why the British are putting so much time, effort and manpower into that area in Kent. Seems to me to be an inordinate amount just for a hoax.'

Vilma knew further debate was futile.

'I want regular updates on Auger, Vilma. I will visit High Command first thing in the morning,' Brietner ordered.

'Very good,' Herr General. Vilma rose to leave.

'And, Vilma, Snapdragon is a hero of the Fatherland. Tread very carefully before you accuse him of being a traitor without firm evidence.'

Vilma bowed his head in acceptance of the reprimand and made for the door.

That night, in an unremarkable semi in southern England, the Great War veteran ex-Captain John Francis Metcalfe suffered a massive heart attack in his sleep. Without ever knowing what hit him, Snapdragon had died instantly.

– CHAPTER TWENTY-EIGHT –

Early morning, Wednesday, September 6th, 1944, 10 Downing Street, London.

'Ah! Morning, Peter,' Churchill greeted as Bushell entered the Cabinet Room. 'There are many things that I loathe about this confounded war, but none more so than these blessed early mornings. I've got a slight change of plan from the military side to tell you about, and then you can fill me in on your latest exploits.'

'I fully expected some fine-tuning from the top brass, Prime Minister. I am no military strategist. The invasion plan I put forward was merely a suggestion, not a recommendation.'

'Just to recap, Peter, the invasion fleet was to make its way across the Dover straight, heading for Calais and then, at a given moment, swing south westward towards Normandy. Now instead of coming over en masse, as it were, there will be a vanguard in front of the main body. This will consist of the bulk of the navy warships we were going to deploy on A-Day, plus a few troop carriers. The warship fleet will contain the three destroyers that are equipped with the new radar. The type 22 U-boats will be duty-bound to attack the leading vessels as they represent the greatest threat. But the new radar-carrying destroyers won't be the only shock they are in for. The troop carriers will be our trump card. They will not be carrying troops at all, but naval personnel, and the vessels will be armed to the gunwales with hundreds of depth charge launchers. At the first sign of submarine attack, along with the warships, they will saturate the area with hundreds of depth charges. The cruisers and battleships will pound Calais from maximum range, and the Germans will be convinced the invasion is heading there. Meanwhile, the main force will have turned southwest at a much earlier time, and hopefully be well on its way to Normandy before it is discovered. The vanguard will turn for Normandy before it gets too close to Calais, and will then become the rear gunners for the convoy. It does leave the main body of vessels perilously short of protection, and the vanguard will inevitably sustain heavy casualties, but if they can occupy, or even perhaps account for a few of those type 22s, then the gamble is definitely worth the risk.'

Bushell seemed impressed. He nodded his approval and smiled. 'I guess that's why they pay these guys the big bucks, Prime Minister.'

'So, was your Kentish jaunt successful?' Churchill enquired.

'Well, we certainly put on a convincing act, Prime Minister. Anybody watching would certainly think we were planning a major project. But our main concern is *was* anybody watching? As you know, Prime Minister, we fear that our main double agent, Snapdragon, may have been discovered. But our site visit was duly reported back to the Abwehr by an agent unknown.'

'So what is the next step, Peter?'

'More deliveries are scheduled over the next couple of days, Prime Minister, including a large consignment of miners' helmets and lamps and what is hopefully our most convincing prop yet, a job lot of individual breathing units.'

'Is there such a thing, Peter?' Churchill asked.

'Not that we are aware of, Prime Minister, but there's one thing the Germans do not do, and that is underestimate our ingenuity. Just to draw them a diagram as it were, as soon as they arrive, there will be a string of soldiers from the camp next door queuing up to try them on. The Germans will be left in no doubt of their function.'

'Just out of interest, Peter, are they of any practical use?'

'None whatsoever, Prime Minister. I believe they've been fashioned from the top half of a regulation gas mask, a length of rubber tubing and a standard issue soldier's water canister, painted black.'

Churchill guffawed. 'Well, as long as it convinces your new German friend. Better meet every morning at this time from here on in, Peter. There are sure to be bumps in the road before this one's in the ledger.'

'Without doubt, Prime Minister.'

– CHAPTER TWENTY-NINE –

Mid-morning, Wednesday, September 6th, 1944, Admiralty Building, London.

Covington and Ledbetter met Bushell in the corridor to his office. He poked his head around the communications room door and quickly scanned the room.

'Snapdragon not in yet?' he enquired.

'No, sir,' replied a voice.

'Send him through as soon as he arrives then, would you?'

Clegg joined them as they passed his office door and the quartet gathered around Bushell's desk and he ordered some tea.

'Right, gentlemen, good morning officially. I met with the PM at 0630 as I shall be doing every morning until Auger reaches its conclusion. The PM has been made aware of the situation. Gentlemen, the floor is yours.'

Clegg took the stand first. 'There's no doubt we're putting up a very convincing show, sir. The Abwehr have intercepted our reports, but currently, we cannot guess how far up the food chain the information has gone.'

'I'm pretty certain that Abwehr operatives won't be easily fooled,' Bushell conceded. 'If they take a few snippets upstairs, they'll be accused of wasting their superiors' time. But wait too long until they have rafts of evidence, and they will be lambasted for putting the Reich in danger – they can't win. It's my understanding that relations at that level are not particularly cordial. Precious few of the Abwehr commanders came through the ranks, and they treat each other with suspicion. So, bearing that in mind, gentlemen, let's examine who we're dealing with. Snapdragon is sure, and I concur, that the officer in charge of our case is Colonel Dieter Vilma. He's a top draw operative and will take some convincing. He's already on to us because we know the Germans went back to look for Didier Pascal. Good job they didn't find him. Otherwise, Auger would be dead in the water already. However, the profile of his boss is very much in our favour – General Manuel Brietner. Snapdragon has actually met him on a couple of occasions. He is not a rabid National Socialist but a pretty keen one. He's a glory seeker and a man very prone to overreact. All grist to the mill for us. My guess is that Abwehr has already compiled a fairly large file on Auger and that Brietner is up-to-date with it. So, let's have contributions for Operation Convince.'

Covington volunteered, 'How about if tomorrow, or later today if it's possible, a van bearing the livery of the British Museum turns up at the site? Frank and I can go with it if you wish. We'll grub around for a while. Throw a few boxes of soil in the back of the van and come home. Tonight, as a sort of afterthought at the end of the news, the BBC tells of a find of Roman artefacts in some field in Kent. I could even put a few cherries on top by giving a quote. Something like, "We're not aware of any Roman settlement in this area, but that's what the find is pointing to as most of the artefacts are tools." We could get *The Times* to run the story as well.'

Frank smiled behind his hand and muttered to himself, 'And we all know where you got that idea from!'

'Brilliant!' enthused Bushell. 'To boot, the comment will come from a bona fide Cambridge professor who's an expert in Roman studies! What's more, it will cause them to rethink your involvement in Auger.'

Bushell picked up the phone. 'Ask Cartwright, Simons and Thompson to come in please.'

Footsteps in the corridor heralded the arrival of the trio and they stood in a neat line awaiting instructions.

Bushell scribbled on a scrap piece of paper and asked Cartwright, 'Has Snapdragon called in?'

'No, sir.'

'If he doesn't arrive or make contact by 1200 hours, ring this number. If there's no answer, put an ONA into action immediately. Get Wilcox and Parfitt to act upon the ONA if needed.'

Concern was written all over Bushell's face.

'You two…' said Bushell, pointing alternately to Simons and Thompson. 'Are going on another Kentish jaunt. Go to the British Museum, commandeer one of their vans and head for the field. Jack and Frank will meet you there. Wear clothing suitable for prodding about in the soil.'

The three underlings left to carry out their commander's bidding.

Ledbetter tried to stifle a giggle. He decided from the wide-eyed look he was getting that an explanation was required.

'There doesn't seem to be any red tape thick enough to withstand that industrial-scale pair of scissors you wield!'

Bushell contemplated for a moment and conceded, 'Yes, I suppose this department does have the power to open most doors rather speedily. Never really thought about it. It just goes with the job.'

After their departure, Bushell turned to Covington and Ledbetter.

'Best if you two go by train. They run every half hour to Dover. Be quicker for you and more comfortable. Do what archaeologists do for a couple of hours, then head back. I know in peacetime you'd have a whole team there, meticulously sifting through tons of soil, but this is wartime and the Germans won't suspect a thing. It's perfect.'

Bushell switched to serious mode. He seemed able to change his tone and demeanour to suit the situation at the drop of a hat.

'Jack, Frank, Operation Auger has drawn you into our little family here and I think an explanation regarding Snapdragon is warranted. I don't need to tell you that being an employee of this department carries with it a certain amount of danger. Even more so in the case of field agents like Snapdragon. Contrary to popular belief, we do not regard our people as dispensable. On the contrary, we feel we have a great duty of care toward them. So we operate a kind of watch-over system. Its code name, rather pleasingly, is Mother Hen. Twice a day, between two pre-set time parameters, the field agents just send a short signal to our communications room. It basically means 'I'm still alive'. If we don't hear from Snapdragon by 1200 hours, it will mean he's missed two contact signals. ONA stands for Operative in Need of Assistance.'

Covington and Ledbetter had thus far treated their sabbatical with the CIU as a bit of a game. Entering the secretive world of intelligence had given the pair an unexpected high, and it didn't enter their heads that it could actually be dangerous. But it was a sobering walk to St Pancras station to catch the Dover train.

– CHAPTER THIRTY –

Afternoon, Wednesday, September 6th, 1944, Excavation Site, Dover, England.

Much to their chagrin, the taxi driver refused to drive Covington and Ledbetter across the field for fear of getting stuck. Instead, he decanted them both by the gate.

'Pick us up here at four please,' said Covington curtly. He made his way with Ledbetter through the army camp.

'Where did you come up with the idea of a Roman find then, Jack?' asked Ledbetter, his voice dripping with sarcasm.

'Just came to me in a flash. Guess I'm just prone to inspirational ideas on the spur of the moment.'

'Yeah, right.' Ledbetter grinned.

They followed a squad of soldiers into the site field. They made their way over to where some of their colleagues were playfully trying on the miners' helmets, while a couple of NCOs demonstrated the breathing apparatus. Covington spotted Major Harding and went to greet him.

'What do you make of our boffin's latest gizmo then,

Major?' he asked, waving his hand at a mask-wearing corporal.

'Well let's just hope your German friend's binoculars are not too powerful!'

The two carried on over to the earth bank. They could see Wally and his gang had been hard at work. They stood admiring a newly dug entrance in the bank.

'It's OK. It's safe to go in,' said a voice behind them.

It was Tynwald, flanked by Wally and Burdock. Ledbetter knocked on one of the supporting sleepers with his knuckles, giving its stability a mock test.

He nodded his approval. 'You've been busy.'

'This was not in the job description,' said Burdock ruefully, examining his hands.

Covington appraised Wally of the purpose of their visit and, satisfied with the reason for their presence, took his charges off to continue their part in the deceit. Covington and Ledbetter thought they should do likewise and began grubbing about on the spoil heap. Ledbetter opened a small case he'd brought, took out a couple of trowels and tossed one to Covington. Both knew it was a futile exercise in terms of a serious search, but kept up the pretence until Thompson drove up in the van, 'British Museum' displayed proudly on the side.

Thomson and Simons donned a pair of brown warehouse coats and unloaded half a dozen packing cases from the back of the van. Studiously they sifted through the earth, occasionally putting a supposed item of interest in a bag and giving it to their assistants, who in turn placed it carefully in one of the crates. After an hour or so, Jack looked at his watch and shouted to Ledbetter, '3.45, Frank, we'd better get going.'

They helped load the crates into the van and waved

Thompson and Simons back on their way, walking back to the field gate to await their taxi.

Rather than take a cab, they decided to walk from St. Pancras to the hotel to rid themselves of train travel stiffness.

'Nightcap?' asked Ledbetter.

'I think we deserve one.'

'What was that you slipped into your pocket?'

'Can't be certain, but I think it's a silver denarii. What have you got in yours?'

'Well if it's not the cheek piece from a centurion's helmet, then I'm Caesar's wine merchant.'

'Which you're not.'

'Which I'm not.'

Later that evening, toward the end of the BBC nine o'clock news, Alvar Liddell told the nation of a find of Roman artefacts near Dover. He quoted Jack Covington almost word for word.

Oberst Vilma listened to the broadcast as he did every evening. He was not interested in the mundane happenings on the home front. He was listening intently for any words or small phrases that could be coded messages to agents or underground groups. When he heard about the Roman finds, he laughed out loud and snorted, 'How daft do they think we are?'

In his opulent country house, General Brietner was also tuned in. Breitner could not speak English, so his translator told him of the Kent discovery. Breitner's thought process came to a single conclusion. There's more to this tunnel story than Vilma thinks.

– CHAPTER THIRTY-ONE –

Late afternoon, Weds, September 6th, 1944,
Admiralty Building, London, England.

B ushell sat behind his desk and supposed Covington and Ledbetter's no-show meant they'd gone straight home. He thought about doing likewise. Like every other day, his last act was to check in with communications for any incomings of significance. He picked up his phone and asked for Cartwright. 'Anything to concern me overnight?' he asked.

'No, sir. Wisden dutifully reported the arrival of the equipment and that troops were being instructed in their use. Sir, Wilcox and Parfitt are here. They wish to see you. May I tag along as well?'

'Of course.'

The three shuffled into Bushell's office and stood rather awkwardly.

'Your faces are not those of people bearing glad tidings,' Bushell observed. 'OK, let's have it.'

Wilcox spoke first. 'Snapdragon's car was still in the drive, so we knocked and when there was no answer, we gained entry and found him dead in bed. I have some basic medical training, sir, and it bears all the hallmarks of a heart attack.'

'I immediately called in a military ambulance and told them to take the body to Hammersmith morgue. I phoned ahead and told them to do an immediate post-mortem, and not to reveal the results to anyone but us. I spoke to the pathologist about ten minutes ago, sir, and his initial thoughts were heart attack but he will, of course, conduct a full post-mortem, toxicology tests and what have you.'

There was a respectful moment of silence.

Bushell slowly raised his head and said. 'Well done, you two. Good job. We must keep this totally under wraps. Snapdragon had an older sister who is now dead, but I do believe there are a couple of nephews. They, unfortunately, will have to wait until after the war to discover their uncle is dead, but they will also learn that he was a genuine war hero. I will see to that.'

'Sir, may I?' asked Cartwright.

'Of course, Cartwright, go ahead.'

'Well firstly, just before Snapdragon left last night, he wanted to tell you something, but you were elsewhere. He was listening in as we monitored messages to and from Wisden. Because of the way the messages were phrased, he said he thought he recognised who Wisden might be. Is that possible, sir?'

'Very much so,' Bushell confirmed. 'It was the signature way a single German signaller always messaged that helped us break the enigma code. Did Snapdragon say anything else?'

'Yes, sir. He identified him as possibly an agent codenamed Everest. He's a little-used operative, a sort of reserve.'

'And he's been brought in now because the Germans suspected Snapdragon – makes sense,' Bushell reasoned.

'Just one more thing he said, sir. He was sure Everest was not German. He didn't know what nationality he was, but that he wasn't German.'

'We do have enemies that are not German but have German sympathies – and plenty of them. That means they can hide in plain sight and it makes them all the harder to track down. Despite this, he's the only reliable sender of fake info we have on this side of the Channel. The last thing we want to do is spook him. Wilcox, Parfitt, do all the necessary, would you? Have Snapdragon buried in an unmarked grave, the nearest one to the village of Paulerspury in Northants. That's where he hailed from. Use usual procedures to bypass officialdom. Turn off all services to the house, secure it and bring me the keys. We'll implement a "For let" as soon as practicable.'

Wilcox and Parfitt left, leaving a slightly distressed Cartwright. Bushell anticipated his question.

'Yes, we do need to let the Germans think Snapdragon is still alive and broadcasting.'

Bushell took a bunch of keys from his jacket pocket and unlocked a drawer in his desk. He extracted a sturdy metal box, and choosing another key, he opened the lid. He dextrously fingered his way through some papers. He briefly scanned one of the contents, jotted down the information, and returned the box to the desk drawer. Handing the note to Cartwright, Bushel gave him a string of instructions.

'That is Snapdragon's call sign and frequency when he contacts Germany. Keep it safe. All you need to do is duplicate what Wisden is sending but a shortened version. You can send one now if you like. Tell them about the helmets and the breathing gizmo. Only you don't know it's a breathing apparatus. Just give a loose description and that you observed troops trying them on for size. If they ask any awkward questions, don't reply before speaking to me.'

'Was Snapdragon's German perfect, sir?'

'Yes, why do you ask?'

'Well, so is mine, sir. Even if Snapdragon's German was only slightly below flawless, they would detect it straight away, which would have caused a problem. As it is there isn't one, sir.'

'Good work, Cartwright, well done. Pop off and send that message will you, and check for any incomings? Then you may as well go and I'll see you bright and early in the morning.'

'Will do, sir. Goodnight.'

'Goodnight, Cartwright.'

With that, Bushell made his way home to mourn in silence his friend and colleague of nearly thirty years.

– CHAPTER THIRTY-TWO –

Early morning, Thurs, September 7th, 1944, 10 Downing Street, London, England.

'We're going to have to stop meeting like this,' Churchill greeted affably from amidst a plume of cigar smoke.

Bushell joined in the joke. 'People are already beginning to talk, sir. Should I go first?'

Churchill waved an affirmative hand.

'You will have already heard about the death of our top double agent, codename Snapdragon. Nothing sinister, the pathologist confirmed this morning, an aortic embolism gave way while he was asleep. He would have died instantly.'

'Damned inconvenient though.'

'To be honest, Prime Minister, it doesn't really alter things very much. As you know, we are pretty sure that the Germans were on to Snapdragon, so in effect, Auger would have been his last operation. We only have two days until A-Day, so one of our operatives can continue to send spurious messages acting as Snapdragon for the next forty-eight hours.'

Churchill raised his eyes to the ceiling, mused for a few seconds, and then pointed his cigar butt towards Bushell.

'Worst case scenario, Peter, if this massive armada is halfway across the Channel and not one man or artillery piece has moved from Normandy towards Calais, the consequences are too dire to contemplate. I know we've covered this ground before, Peter, but failure is not an option.'

Bushell sought to allay Churchill's fears.

'If the Germans buy Auger, Prime Minister, the reinforcements from Normandy will have had to begin their journey before our vessels leave port. It's a six-hour trek. They know they have to be in position before the first vessel comes within range. If they swallow the bait, they will know Auger will commence at dawn, so it's my guess the Germans will mobilise soon after dark tomorrow night. We do have a pretty good safety net in place, sir – the Germans don't move, then we don't sail.'

There was evidence of partial satisfaction in Churchill's expression, but it could not conceal an inner concern, nor indeed his battle weariness.

'Let me speak with candour, Peter. Like you, I tire of this war, but the fear of defeat, and the fearful aftermath that would be visited upon the British people should that defeat happen, keeps me going. I have to tell you, Peter, should Auger fail, or even be abandoned, I really don't know where we go next. Any sort of invasion, without some sort of subterfuge to wrong-foot the Germans, will end in wholesale slaughter.'

Bushell had never seen Churchill so downbeat and considered his reply carefully. He concluded that a glass-half-full response was necessary.

'Prime Minister, the Germans are not winning the war. At best, they are delaying its inevitable conclusion. Granted they have been very effective at implementing that delay, but their ability to wage war is being diminished every day. The twenty-four-hour bombing of Germany is creating shortages. We have operatives at work in occupied Europe, who are continually putting spanners in the works. Of course, we must break this status quo, but we still control the board. Whose position would you rather be in, sir – ours or theirs?'

Churchill emitted a trademark chortle. 'I hope to God you are right, Peter. So, onwards and upwards with Auger then. Open every knavish box of tricks in your armoury, unleash the underhanded dogs of war, Auger must succeed!'

'Very Henry the Fifth, Prime Minister,' Bushell encouraged.

'Report to the Cabinet War Rooms at 0900 hours tomorrow, Peter. Bring your full team if needs be. All Allied commanders will be here.'

'I'll be sure to wash behind my ears, Prime Minister.'

– CHAPTER THIRTY-THREE –

Early morning, Thurs, September 7th, 1944, Abwehr HQ, Berlin, Germany.

'Bring me some good news, Max,' said Vilma hopefully as Bierhoff entered his office, bearing two cups of coffee.

'Well, I do have lots to report, Herr Oberst. It's up for debate whether it's good or not. The BBC informs us that Roman remains have been found at the Kent site, Herr Oberst.'

Vilma nodded. 'Brietner was on the scrambler to me as soon as the broadcast had finished. He hinted, not very subtly, that I should take more seriously the existence of this tunnel.'

'In that case, Herr Oberst, I'm afraid I've got more grist to the general's mill. The earthworks in Kent now has what appears to be a tunnel entrance, shored up with railway sleepers. Also, a fleet of lorries delivered dozens of packing crates, some containing miners' helmets, as well as what appears to be some sort of modified gas masks.'

'Did both Snapdragon and Everest report these goings on?'

'Yes, Herr Oberst.'

'Speak, Max,' Vilma cajoled, noticing Bierhoff rubbing his chin.

'I think you may be right about Snapdragon, Herr Oberst. After a few years in this place, you get a feeling for things, especially if it doesn't seem right. There's nothing tangible or provable – just a gut feeling.'

'Go on, Max.'

'A British Museum van arrived at the site yesterday morning, no doubt to whisk away artefacts ostensibly found by workmen. It's how Snapdragon and Everest both reported the same scenario. We know Everest is in the area but we actually don't know for sure that Snapdragon is. Snapdragon reported the presence of the van a full hour before Everest did. If Snapdragon is being told what to report and when to report it, a Whitehall operative may have jumped the gun.'

'And called it in before the van had actually arrived,' mulled Vilma.

'There's more, Herr Oberst. Their reports on the contents of the crates differ. Everest just described them as helmets and gas masks, which from several hundred metres away would be as much as you could make out. Snapdragon assumedly was no closer, yet was far more detailed. He specifically described the helmets as miners' helmets, i.e. something you'd wear underground. He doesn't even mention the word gas mask, but describes them as some sort of breathing apparatus.'

'In other words, ensuring we are in no doubt what they are up to.'

'Quite so, Herr Oberst. Everest said two men arrived by taxi shortly after the museum van and joined two other men on site. All four sifted through the spoil heap. Almost certainly the four were Covington, Ledbetter and their two stand-ins.'

'Almost certainly,' Vilma agreed.

'Snapdragon knows Covington and Ledbetter and their alter egos, yet he doesn't mention them by name or even acknowledge their presence. He also did not report the van's departure, which Everest did. Herr Oberst, Snapdragon is sending information from Kent when it looks fairly conclusive that he isn't there.'

'I agree, Max, but I doubt the general will see it that way. He will say that Snapdragon is an experienced operative and there will be good reasons for his behaviour. Any more suspicions from your inner-self, Max?'

'Not from mine, Herr Oberst, but Lieutenant Muller thinks he may have picked up on something. Muller is one of our most experienced radio operators and has picked up thousands of messages from Snapdragon and knows his signature better than anyone.'

'Go on, Max,' Vilma encouraged

'Yes, Herr Oberst. As you know, no two people send Morse code the same – it's like a fingerprint. Operators learn to recognise agents by their signature and Muller is sure that over the last couple of days' messages, purportedly from Snapdragon, have not been sent by him. Muller has also detected very minor changes in wording. The German is almost too perfect.'

'But that doesn't make any sense, Max. Even if they suspect that we know he's a British double agent, he's safely in their care so why not let him send his own messages?'

'We simply don't know, Herr Oberst. Could be a simple explanation. He may be unwell. Or could be something more sinister.'

Vilma pondered for a few seconds and switched to grandmaster mode. He concluded there was more to this game than worrying about one minor piece. Bierhoff read his mind.

'Planning your next move, Herr Oberst?'

'I've just removed a pawn from the board, Max. Snapdragon may or may not be a double agent, but what he is in this moment in time is an irrelevance.'

'Before you formulate any new operation, Herr Oberst, may I conclude the messages? They may have some bearing on your thoughts.'

'Carry on, Max.'

'Radio traffic is on the increase between resistance units in the Calais area and further afield. Much of it is chatter about Saturday the ninth being A-Day, so we can now take that as read. However, we keep picking up a cipher of letters and numbers. We think it may be a map reference. We are trying to decode it now and should have some sort of results by lunchtime.'

'Care to hazard a guess where this map reference will pinpoint?'

'It can only be one of two things in my mind. Possible drop zone for paratroops or the entrance to the tunnel. If it's a largish area then it's a drop zone, if it's a few square metres, then it's the tunnel entrance. Speaking of which, Herr Oberst, our searches in the area for people who may possibly know the whereabouts of the small hill in Covington's photo have borne some fruit. You will recall Juste Gilbert, the amateur archaeologist who met with Covington in 1939?'

'The now deceased Monsieur Gilbert.'

'Indeed, Herr Oberst. But his elder brother is still alive, a retired teacher. Our operatives in Calais believe he still lives in the area and should not be too difficult to track down.'

'Send some more operatives in to help, Max. Time is now of the essence. I trust your judgement that the cypher is a map reference. I would assume that this is where the resistance is trying to make us look for a fictitious hole in the ground.'

'I'll see to it right away, Herr Oberst. I have already dispatched Hauptmann Franck and Leutnant Rindt to the area to oversee proceedings. What's our next move?'

'Well, the general wants regular updates so, for good or ill, that's what he's going to get. If he doesn't mention Snapdragon then neither will I, but I will stress that if we can find both this map reference and locate this damned hillock, then once and for all we'll be able to dismiss Auger as a hoax. We need those two pieces of information, Max, and we need them quickly. Lean on a few people. Pay for the information if you need to. I'm doing battle on two fronts here.'

'The general and the Allies,' Bierhoff agreed.

'Yes,' said Vilma ruefully, 'and all the latest information I'm about to feed him will only stoke the fires of his zeal to believe this rubbish. It's too late to nip this in the bud, Max, but we still have a window of opportunity to prevent it flowering into a full scale disaster. It's time for Rubliov, Max – it's time to attack.'

Bierhoff moved his weight uneasily from one foot to the other as he listlessly gathered his papers. Vilma sensed the disquiet and without raising his eyes from the desk uttered slowly.

'Max, get it off your chest before you explode.'

'I'm sorry, Herr Oberst, but part of my remit in this organisation is to give the perspective from the point of view of a senior army officer.'

'Indeed it is, Max. What is your military mind telling you?'

'Well, to a degree, it doesn't matter whether the tunnel exists or it doesn't, Herr Oberst. The simple facts are these… If High Command moves the men and artillery north, the Allies will come. If nothing moves, neither will the Allies. We all know a second invasion is coming, but no army in its right mind would launch an attack on this scale having first given the enemy a week's notice of when and where.'

'Would seem pretty foolhardy,' Vilma agreed.

'But my biggest concern is this, Herr Oberst. The evidence you're about to put before General Brietner is far from conclusive, but that's not my worry. Herr Oberst, the British to my mind have definitely changed tack since we discovered things we were not supposed to, the aerial maps for instance. They are using a sort of reverse psychology, trying to convince us that Auger is an elaborate hoax to cover up the fact that the tunnel does actually exist. Herr Oberst, you and I, and Oberleutnant Schwartz for that matter, are convinced that this tunnel is as likely to exist as a unicorn. But if your assessment of the general's thought processes are correct, and I've no doubt that they are, and he comes to the same conclusion about the hoax being a cover up, he will take that as conclusive evidence that the tunnel does exist and Auger is for real.'

Vilma nodded in agreement. 'His thought processes might be blinkered, Max, but he is nobody's fool. I think the best course of action is to lay everything before him and stress the point we are close to discovering if a sub-Channel tunnel does emerge in France. At least that should buy us some time. You carry on your hunt for map references and history teachers, Max, and I'll go and appraise Breitner of the Allies latest attempts to con us. Just one more thing, Max: part of the Rubliov gambit is to make a sudden surprise move to confuse your opponent. Cut off all contact with Snapdragon, and don't send any messages or acknowledge anything he sends us. Not only will the British conclude that we've rumbled Snapdragon, but it will also sow a seed of doubt that we may be onto Auger as well.'

With that, both gathered up their separate papers and left.

Vilma sat uneasily in his chair while General Brietner digested all the latest data he and Bierhoff had compiled. His worst fears were about to be realised.

'Vilma, you are still completely convinced that Operation Auger is a hoax?' Breitner asked, his voice loaded with suspicion.

'We have no hard evidence that the tunnel exists, Herr General. In fact, we hope to prove its non-existence very soon.'

'Yes,' Breitner muttered doubtfully. 'So, how do you account for the massive concentrations of troops gathering at ports around Dover, looking for all the world that they are about to embark? Your own aerial reconnaissance tells us that.'

'They have to make the invasion look real, Herr General. And the invasion will be for real if we move masses of artillery pieces and thousands of troops from Normandy to Calais.'

'And you think that if we just stand and do nothing, the Allies will do likewise, Vilma?'

'That's our assessment, Herr General. For the time

being they will not launch an invasion because they've told us they are coming and where they intend to land.'

'I still think you are missing the point, Vilma,' Brietner argued stubbornly. 'Why would the Allies go to all this trouble just to possibly do nothing?'

'There's one more thing that makes us highly suspicious, Herr General.'

'Go on, Vilma.'

'It's all been too easy, Herr General. We've almost been spoon-fed the information. Couple that with mistakes they've made and it just reeks of deception.'

Breitner leapt to his feet. 'And that is your mistake, Vilma!' he said forcefully. 'Don't you see, they've made it easy to convince you it's a hoax when it is anything but! It's all part of the plan.'

Vilma's heart sank. *Damn, he's fallen headlong into it*, he thought.

'You said earlier that you were close to proving the non-existence of the tunnel? I will need positive proof by 0900 hours tomorrow. Meanwhile, I will meet with the High Command and recommend they ask the Führer's permission to bring at least two artillery brigades and three divisions to stand by, ready to move to Calais to repel a second invasion. Army patrols are very infrequent in the rural parts of France. We don't have the troops to spare, but I will order more frequent patrols, even if it is with fewer men in each section. Any unusual activity they come across, they will be ordered to take no action, but observe only and report to the Abwehr. You will order all your operatives to do likewise. Keep me informed, Vilma, hourly if necessary.'

– CHAPTER THIRTY-FOUR –

Mid-morning, Thurs, September 7th, 1944, Admiralty Building, London, England.

Bushell made the short walk from Downing Street to Whitehall and pondered how much more pleasant it was than four years earlier. The threat of invasion had virtually disappeared. Air raids had ceased and with them the barrage balloons and the sandbags from in front of every official doorway. There were more people on the streets and they were now more apt to wear a smile. London was beginning to look a lot less like a city under siege. *If only they knew*, Bushell thought, *that five minutes ago I had to give a slightly depressed prime minister a pep talk.*

As he entered the Admiralty Building, Bushell let all such flowery sentiments float from his brain, and by the time he opened the door to his office, he was in fully switched on intelligence mode. Waiting for him were the quartet of Covington, Ledbetter, Clegg and Cartwright.

'Good morning, gentlemen,' Bushell greeted. 'Right, to business. We have a meeting with the PM tomorrow morning at Sparrow Chirp and all of Allied command will be there. It is important that Auger is proceeding as expected. So, today we need to ramp up the convincers. But let's see where we are now. John?'

'Well, Commander,' Clegg replied, 'the resistance has done a sterling job. They've filled the airways with all kinds of Auger-related messages. The Germans have almost certainly picked them up and deduced what A-Day is and when it's going to launch. The resistance has radioed their units in the area passing on a map reference for the explosion that will expose the tunnel entrance. It's very loosely coded, so if the Abwehr are on the ball they will decode it quickly, if they haven't already.'

Bushell nodded approvingly. 'How large an area does the map reference cover?'

'The last number was deliberately omitted from both the Northings and the Eastings,' Clegg continued. 'And the area is about an acre in size. So, when the extra digit is known, this will narrow it down to a few square yards. The resistance will broadcast that information late tomorrow evening.'

Covington's and Ledbetter's puzzled expressions prompted Bushell to relieve their perplexity.

'The last thing we want is for the Germans to discover the exact location of where the tunnel emerges in France. A few hours of excavation will show that no such entrance exists, convincing evidence that Auger is a hoax. It would take a week to prospect an acre or so, a week the Germans don't have. Actually, pinpointing the spot at the last minute gives extra authenticity to the ruse. It's what the Germans would expect. How are the resistance doing with their pyrotechnics?'

Clegg glanced at Cartwright, willing him to speak. Cartwright obliged the prompt.

'The explosives to simulate the blowing of the tunnel entrance were planted a week ago, sir. Just in case the Germans do go poking around, they're not exactly where the map reference says the entrance will be. Unlikely, especially when they have the last two digits, it will be pitch dark, and only a few hours from the launch of Auger. About ten minutes after the main explosion, a whole series of thunder flashes and other fireworks will ignite in the area and, coupled with some trigger-happy Frenchmen discharging their weapons willy-nilly in the same parish, the Germans will think two divisions have popped out of the tunnel.'

Ledbetter grinned. 'The Germans will then know there's an entrance to the tunnel on the English side of the Channel and an exit on the French side. What they won't know is that it hasn't got a middle bit.'

'Bit of a drawback,' agreed Bushell. 'But we are missing the point here somewhat. All this Guy Fawkes stuff is all well and good, but this will only happen if the Germans have swallowed the bait, and the troops and ordnance are well on the way to Calais, if not in situ. At the moment, on a scale of one to ten, we have no idea if we are at one or nine in forcing the German's hand. We need a crackerjack trump card to tip the balance. The floor is open, gentlemen.'

Before anyone could proffer any suggestions, a phone rang rudely on Bushell's desk. 'Bushell,' he identified, listening intently. 'He'll be right along.' Bushell replaced the receiver.

'Young Wilcox seems quite excited, Cartwright. Important messages await your attention. Go and see what the cause of his delirium is, would you, and report straight back? We'll pause this meeting until you return.

Thinking about it, bring Wilcox, Simons and Parfitt along as well – the more eyes we have looking at this the better.'

– CHAPTER THIRTY-FIVE –

Late morning, Thurs, September 7th, 1944. Abwehr HQ, Berlin, Germany.

Vilma idly clicked a pencil up and down between his teeth as he sat in his chair. He was worried that General Brietner was close to sending Wehrmacht's western land forces on a fool's errand, a manoeuvre which would have no historical military equivalent in terms of stupidity. Bierhoff entered and snapped his train of thought.

'Good news, Herr Oberst,' Bierhoff enthused. 'We've found Juste Gilbert's brother. He's in a nursing home suffering from a combination of bombing raid injuries and old age. But he's fully cognisant mentally, though too frail to be removed from the hospital. A couple of operatives are hurrying there with copies of Covington's maps and photos.'

'Excellent, Max, what about the map reference?'

'There, Herr Oberst, it's a good news/bad news scenario. Our decoders have translated the cipher and it is indeed a map reference. An initial search places it in an area of bare land about two kilometres outside of

Calais. The bad news is the last digit of the latitude and longitude grid reference is missing. Therefore, the area we're looking at is about one hectare as opposed to a few square metres. The omission is no doubt deliberate, Herr Oberst.'

'An omission that will no doubt be rectified late when it's too late for us to do anything about it,' Vilma remarked ruefully. 'The missing two numbers are a supposed security element to protect the resistance. This, I believe, is yet another British convincer, or at least an attempted one. Is there anything within that hectare of French countryside, a feature of some sort, that could remotely resemble a tunnel entrance, Max?'

'I've sent in a couple of operatives to reconnoitre the area, Herr Oberst. Should we cordon off the area?'

'No, Max, remember we are under orders to observe only. I'm pretty certain that all they will find is a flat piece of countryside where the only thing resembling a tunnel entrance will be a molehill. Max, the British are trying to keep us guessing. But which category does it fall into, the "It's a hoax to cover up the reality of Operation Auger" or "Auger is for real and no hoax is being enacted"? Any ideas, Max?'

'Bearing in mind that we both think that it's ninety-nine point nine per cent certain the tunnel does not exist, then there are three scenarios. One it's a concocted hoax to cover up a real operation. Two, there is no "hoax" hoax and we have stumbled upon a real operation. Lastly, the whole thing is a real hoax – and all the smart money is firmly on number three. A few hours with a couple of mechanical shovels will prove all three to be no more than figments of British Intelligence imagination. The problem is, we don't know where to dig, and it's unlikely we are going to know by 0900 hours tomorrow. Could you persuade the General to give us until at least 1700 hours?'

'I can but try, Max, but may I remind you again, we are under orders to observe only, so no digging. I have a horrible feeling that when I send this lot up to him, he's going to be even more convinced that it's the first item on your list of possibilities, the concocted hoax. And he'll take the map reference as proof positive of the same – to distract us from where the real entrance is. Anything else, Max?'

'Saving the most interesting until last, Herr Oberst. Something came in via diplomatic route from the Spanish embassy in London. In our business, your axiom of "Examine every detail, study every move" is worthy of bearing in mind at all times. But even in our line of work, things occasionally drop into your lap.'

Vilma was intrigued, 'And what's this particular gift horse, Max?' he asked.

'Well, I'm not sure how to describe it, Herr Oberst. Good luck, right place, right time, synchronicity, probably a combination of all of them. Yesterday, some medical students were assisting the coroner at Hammersmith morgue. A military ambulance arrived and two soldiers brought in a body. The coroner asked the students to leave as he had to conduct the post-mortem on it alone due to security reasons.'

Vilma raised his hand, 'Two questions, Max. How did we come by this information and of what interest is it to us?'

'A little later, the same students were drinking in a public house in Chelsea with some of their colleagues and were relating the story, laughing, about the body of a spy being brought into the morgue. This pub is just around the corner from the Spanish embassy, and is often frequented by embassy staff, many of whom are sympathetic to our cause.'

'And they have diplomatic immunity, so can wander about London unmolested,' Vilma pointed out.

'Indeed, Herr Oberst, and one such "friend" was present at the time and the word "spy" made him prick up his ears and he began to take mental notes.'

'Yes, Max, but did he overhear anything useful?'

'He most certainly did, Herr Oberst. The students caught a glimpse of the body and told their colleagues it was a middle-aged man, still in his pyjamas. One student also noticed the end of the little finger on his left hand was missing. What added fuel to the fire was that one of the soldiers announced on entering the morgue that they had "brought the body from Mettlesham, we believe you are expecting it". As soon as the students left, our sharp-eared Spaniard returned to the embassy and forwarded it on to us.'

'Good god, Max, it has to be Snapdragon. What's more, if they were taking the body for a post-mortem, it means the British don't know how he died. Still being in his pyjamas indicates dying in his sleep, which points to natural causes.'

'I think this proves once and for all your theory that Snapdragon was a double agent, Herr Oberst,' Beirhoff pointed out. 'The last contact we had from him was sent several hours after he died.'

'Unfortunately, Max, his untimely demise denies us the chance to prove it one hundred per cent – at least in the eyes of Breitner.'

Bierhoff bore his worried look again. 'I know it was our air reconnaissance that discovered the earthworks and troop build up in Kent, Herr Oberst, but it was Snapdragon that first alerted us to Operation Auger and connected the two. To my mind, if Snapdragon was a double agent, then that's conclusive proof Auger is a complete hoax.'

'I agree, Max, but I doubt Breitner will buy it. I'll ship this lot upstairs and will no doubt be summoned forthwith.'

'Will you tell him about Snapdragon, Herr Oberst?'

Vilma shook his head. 'I won't include it in these latest reports, but I will tell him at our next meeting, which I estimate will be about five minutes after he's read them. The question of "is or isn't he a double agent" is irrelevant now, and I don't need to try and convince Breitner. I'll point out Muller's suspicions about Snapdragon's signature and how we believe a body delivered to a London mortuary is that of Snapdragon. However, we're behind the eight ball again, Max. Proving Snapdragon was a double agent may have been the only way we had to prove Auger is a hoax.'

– CHAPTER THIRTY-SIX –

Late morning, Thursday, September 7th, 1944, Admiralty Building, London, England.

Cartwright returned to Bushell's office with Wilcox, Simons and Parfitt all in tow. Bushell drained his coffee cup and bade Cartwright take the floor.

'What news, young Cartwright?'

Cartwright could hardly contain himself. 'Firstly, sir, we think the Germans may be on to Snapdragon, not his passing, sir, but that he's a double agent. I have sent several messages this morning and sent another just now. None have been acknowledged or replied to.'

Bushell gave a resigned shrug. 'After the errors we made over Jack's photos and the Lysander debacle, I suppose it was only a matter of time. Right, so let's not make this easy for them. If we stop sending messages, it will just confirm their suspicions. Are we still monitoring traffic between Wisden and the Abwehr?'

Cartwright nodded confirmation.

'Keep duplicating everything Wisden sends, but just vary it a bit. Tell you what, report the arrival of another convoy of lorries. The Germans won't know if it's true, or that Wisden may have just missed it. Should confuse them anyway.'

Covington tentatively raised his hand to catch Bushell's eye.

'Jack?'

'If this convoy of lorries is fictitious, why not fabricate an inventory of goods they are bearing? There are industrial-size generators and air pumps already on site. Why not have delivery of miles of cable and rubber piping – even some canaries!'

'Splendid, Jack!' Bushell said, beaming. 'It's certainly equipment that would be of use in such an operation. Even though it's imaginary, the Germans don't know that, and it will add a seed of doubt that Snapdragon is still active and doing his job, even if they are not quite sure for whom. See to it straight after the meeting, would you, Cartwright? Carry on.'

'The Germans have sent quite a few operatives into the Calais area, specifically looking for local historians, teachers, academics, museum workers, and students. Our best guess is that they are trying to find Mr Covington's small hill and possibly checking out exactly where the map reference is.'

Bushell grimaced and spoke with a note of trepidation in his voice.

'The latter doesn't overly concern me. The former certainly does. I have no doubt they are trying to locate Jack's man-made hillock and should they do so, excavate it and find no trace of a tunnel entrance. Well, that's another box ticked in proving the non-existence of said tunnel.'

Covington felt compelled to speak. 'If I may,

Commander, the Germans are going to need a massive slice of luck to find anyone who recognises the hillock, let alone knows its location. It was an extraordinary set of circumstances that led me to it in the first place. Moreover, it's in the middle of nowhere and, despite being quite close to Calais, it's surrounded by scrubland. It's off the beaten track and quite difficult to get to. I can't see anyone being able to recognise it from some grainy aerial photos and a two-thousand-year-old Roman map, and the only person who could have led them to it is dead.'

'And time is on our side,' Bushell concurred. 'Nevertheless, it does not relieve us of the problem of having to come up with a killer blow that has the German High Command convinced Auger is going to happen. Gentlemen, the floor is yours.'

Ledbetter spoke up, 'Commander, Jack and I are new to all this. Could you be a bit more specific as to what you are looking for?'

'I'll try, Frank. Everything that the Germans would expect to happen in the thirty-six hours before a massive seaborne invasion. Tomorrow, tens of thousands of troops will begin to embark onto hundreds of vessels. An armada of navy warships will congregate in the Channel off Dover, ready for escort duty. But our objective is to make the Germans move thousands of men and scores of artillery pieces and tanks from Normandy to Calais. They will not do that unless they are one hundred per cent certain that the invasion is going to happen, backed up by hundreds of Allied soldiers popping out of the ground behind their lines. All that German armour needs to be on the move before a ship sets sail. And thus far we have not done enough to convince them to do that.'

'So we need to pull one final rabbit out of the hat then. Is that what you're saying?' asked Ledbetter.

'I'm not going to beat about the bush, gentlemen. It has to be some rabbit and some hat, as Churchill said to me. I'm sure there is enough IQ of the devious variety in this room to accomplish the fate.'

The combined thought process was interrupted by the phone ringing.

'Take that, would you?' asked Bushell, looking at Cartwright. Cartwright obliged and picked up the receiver. The sober look on his face told everyone the conversation was highly important. He studiously replaced the receiver in its cradle.

'Well, Commander,' he announced, 'the rabbit and the hat may not need to be quite as big as first thought. Radio monitors stationed near the frontline in Normandy have picked up a message from German High Command to General von Rundstedt's HQ. Multiple artillery regiments, tank brigades and army divisions have been put on standby in readiness to move.'

No one in the room uttered the word 'Wow' but everyone felt like it. Bushell immediately reinstated decorum. 'Cartwright, get on the scrambler to number 10, give the PM my compliments. Pass on that message, will you, and inform Eisenhower at Camp Griffiss.'

Cartwright hurriedly left the office and Bushell quickly brought everyone back down to earth.

'OK, gentlemen. The size of the rabbit may have diminished slightly, but we're still a long way off extracting it from the hat. This last message conveys nothing more than preparation. It's a long way from confirmation. We still need the knockout punch.'

Ledbetter thought it was time he made a contribution.

187

He half-raised his hand, as if seeking permission to speak. Bushell raised his eyebrows toward him to give him the go-ahead.

'Commander, this knockout punch you're looking for, is it the final convincer for which ploy? The "convince them it's a hoax to cover up what we're trying to do" or the one where we're "trying to keep the operation a secret but letting them know about it anyway"? Bearing in mind, of course, that both elements are hoaxes.'

'Either, or combinations thereof. Why, what have you in mind, Frank?'

'Well, I'm not saying I can deliver a knockout blow, but I think I may be able to put us well ahead on points. Please feel free to shoot me down if I get anything wrong here. All the troop build up around Dover, ready for the invasion, is there for all to see. We don't need to tell the Germans about that. Because of the Snapdragon situation, the Germans are highly sceptical of any messages we send regarding Auger, likewise any radio traffic they pick up from the resistance, but nonetheless, they are still duty bound to investigate it.' Ledbetter scanned the faces in the room and buoyed by the expressions of broad agreement, he continued. 'So my suggestion would be, take the subterfuge to the other side of the Channel to where the Germans can see it.'

Bushell seemed intrigued. 'And how,' he asked, 'will this overt display of chicanery manifest itself?'

'Well, I think we need to ramp up the divide between the hoax hoax and the real hoax, and have the two tunnel entrances front and centre of the disunity. Step up the convincers that the kosher tunnel is the one referred to in the map reference. Tomorrow morning, have the resistance send a gang of workmen, complete with mechanical shovels, to the wider area of the map reference. Purportedly they are there to carry out some sort of civil engineering work. Overnight, park a couple of suspicious-looking lorries near the site. Camouflage them well enough that they look camouflaged, but not well enough that the Germans can't spot them.'

Cartwright seemed unconvinced. 'Surely the Germans will just roll up and see what the French are up to? Then what?'

'No, no they won't,' contradicted Bushell. 'Firstly, apart from the troops manning the coastal defences, who will all be at the ready for action stations, the Germans are very thin on the ground around Calais. Most of the Wehrmacht is busy bottling up our forces in Normandy. Secondly, the Germans are desperate for Auger to happen. They think we don't know that they know. They want to be in position to decimate our soldiers as they emerge from the tunnel. Therefore, any troops or agents in the area will be under orders to observe only.'

Parfitt scratched the top of his head and looked quizzically at Ledbetter. 'Where does the other tunnel come into your plan? Presumably, we want them to think that the thus far undiscovered hillock is the other alternative and that it's still in the game.'

'Indeed. But the reference to that entrance must be sparse. Just enough not to dismiss it completely. Then from tomorrow, get the resistance to start referring to the entrance where all the activity is as "entrance one" or give it a codename. Then later on, mention sporadically another code name that can only refer to a second entrance.'

'I'm impressed thus far,' Bushell enthused. 'What about you, John?'

'So far, so good,' Clegg agreed. 'But like you, Commander, I think we need a little bit more to tip the Germans over the edge.'

Bushell too felt they were close to achieving what was needed and thought some clarification of their aims might just produce another idea.

'Gentlemen, in earlier discussions I talked briefly about the Abwehr, our opponents in this game of deception and fraud, and formidable opponents they are too. I have made mention of Colonel Vilma, who to all intents and purposes runs the Abwehr. He is an excellent operative. But he does have an Achilles heel and it's called General Brietner. His boss. Brietner is first and foremost a soldier, a Nazi and a glory seeker. This plays straight into our hands. Everything the Abwehr has on Auger will end up on Brietner's desk and I have no doubt, his interpretation of it will differ markedly from Vilma's. Brietner has already persuaded the German High Command – and ipso facto Hitler – of the clear and present threat Auger possesses. Hence the order to all those troops in Normandy to prepare to move. What I'm saying, gentlemen, is that it's Brietner we have to convince, not the Abwehr necessarily. And we now know that he has an itchy trigger finger, so that does make our job slightly easier. But make no mistake, the Abwehr, and Vilma in particular, will do their damnedest to persuade Brietner that such action is foolhardy.'

Ledbetter's contribution had also impressed Covington. Their long association had seen them frequently think along the same lines, even occasionally going as far as finishing each other's sentences. He believed he had the perfect addition to Ledbetter's plan.

It was slightly outlandish and he was not sure it was doable. *Only one way to find out*, he thought.

'Commander, is there some means by which we can get a message to the Abwehr? Not from a British or German agent, either real or imagined, nor picked up from resistance radio traffic, but from a German radio operative on the ground near Calais. Oh, and would it be possible to make a parachute drop to the resistance ASAP?'

Bushell looked to his staff for some sort of help. Cartwright obliged. 'The only way we can get a German radio operator to send a message is to give him something worthy of reporting.'

'And what or whom, may I ask, Jack, would you like us to parachute into France?' Bushell asked.

'A dozen British sapper's uniforms,' said Covington, silencing the room. They could not have been more stunned if he'd said a dozen eggs.

'I can't wait for your explanation, Jack!' Bushell said with a laugh. Covington obliged.

'Well, there's no way a large army of soldiers would be sent through this tunnel without blindly knowing what is on the other side. The tunnel may collapse. It could be flooded. So the only way would be to send through a small expeditionary force first, and who better than a dozen sappers? If you can rope in the resistance's help here, get a dozen of them to dress up in uniforms, and along with a few of their mates acting as guides, suddenly appear out of the undergrowth near where Frank's workmen will be. If, as you say, the area will be being keenly watched, the Germans will be sure to clock them. I'd say a dozen British sappers on the loose in the French countryside would be worth reporting, wouldn't you? Once they've wandered around long enough to make sure they've been seen, they can melt into the surrounding woods, change back into their civvies and burn the uniforms.'

'Jack, that *is* hideously brilliant!' beamed Bushell.

Covington was on a roll. 'The result of the ploy should be threefold. Firstly, it will convince the Germans that we're acting out a hoax to cover up that Auger is for real. Second, they are looking in the wrong place for the tunnel entrance. Lastly, the tunnel actually exists. I would add one caveat though. The Germans are sure to go looking for the tunnel entrance, and we don't want them stumbling on the hillock by accident. The hillock is to the north of the map reference area, so if the pseudo-sappers could appear from the west that would be good. It would make sense anyway, because it's nearer to the sea. Timing is of the essence as well. I'd say around 1400 hours. There will be plenty of daylight for them to be seen, but by the time the message has got to Berlin, acted upon, and orders come back to inaugurate a search, there'll only be a couple of hours of daylight left.'

Bushell swayed back in his chair and laughed.

'Jack, Frank, I have a confession to make. I told you when you first walked through my door that it was your academic expertise I craved, but that was only half the story. I knew your background and the adversity you both encountered in your upbringing. You both used your determined mindset to not only overcome that adversity but coupled it with hard work and massive intellect to rise to the very top of your chosen professions. I had a gut feeling that you would be a great asset to this department in a wider capacity. You have both surpassed those expectations by a massive degree.'

There was a polite, spontaneous round of applause. Parfitt gave a little shake of his head and smiled.

'What's the matter, Parfitt, afraid you might lose your job?' Bushell asked affably.

'Indeed, sir, that and a general feeling of inadequacy.' Everyone laughed agreeably.

'Right, to business,' Bushell ordered. 'Jack, I'm not going to parachute your sapper uniforms in. Too many things could go wrong. Cartwright, where is that resistance liaison officer? Captain Dupont, is it? Where can he be found?'

'I believe he's in the building, sir, waiting to make his contribution to Auger.'

'Right, go and seek him out and fetch him down here, would you? Parfitt, Simons, requisition a car and get to Chelsea Barracks. Use your accreditation and pilfer twelve sapper's uniforms and twelve pairs of boots, sizes various. Get yourselves back here as quickly as you can. Make sure you have enough juice to get to Hendon Airfield and back. Wilcox, contact Hendon Airfield and book a Lysander and pilot. Be ready for take-off around dusk for a drop-off in France. John, get hold of Major Harding at the Kent field, will you? Tell him I want a dozen soldiers going into the tunnel entrance. They must be in full kit and that includes wearing the miner's helmets and the breathing apparatus. Late afternoon will be fine, as long as there's enough light for prying eyes to see it. They can come out again as soon as it's dark of course.'

Bushell sat down to draw breath, both figuratively and actually. There was a few seconds hiatus while the lower ranks left the room to act upon their instructions. Bushell felt he needed to tell Covington why he'd tweaked his plan.

'Jack, I assume your plan included informing the resistance of their part in it by wireless message. This would involve quite a long transmission due to the intricate plans and timings. The longer the transmission, the more chance of it being intercepted. Couple that with a parachute drop, which is another inexact science, and there are too many things that could have gone wrong. We'll pack the uniforms into a Lysander, and hand them straight over to the resistance along with a Frenchman who will explain exactly what is wanted, face-to-face. Doesn't lessen the brilliance of your great idea though.'

Ledbetter waved the apology away. 'No explanation necessary, Commander. We'll come up with the ideas, you handle the logistics.'

Again Bushell couldn't help but grin. He realised that Covington and Ledbetter were good for him spiritually as well as professionally. He enjoyed their company. Cartwright returned, closely followed into the office by Captain Dupont.

'Thanks for coming, Captain Dupont,' Bushell greeted. He proceeded to explain both parts of the Covington/Ledbetter plan and how it would involve about twenty resistance fighters. They all moved to the map room and Bushell asked Cartwright to indicate the area corresponding to the map reference.

'Is there a safe landing zone nearby?' Bushell asked.

'Several,' Dupont confirmed. 'We'll use this one. It's a bit further away from Calais.'

'While we are here,' Bushell mused, 'roughly where is your little hillock, Jack?'

Covington stabbed the map with his forefinger. 'I need a larger scale map to be accurate,' Covington reasoned.

'Bushell glanced at his watch. 'Parfitt and Simons should be back in about forty-five minutes. So, Captain, if you would accompany Cartwright here to the radio room, you can message your contact to tell them you'll be paying them a visit. Don't say anything else over the airwaves, except perhaps it may be useful if your reception committee consisted of at least two fairly high-ranking members of the resistance. Cuts down the need for passing orders up the line. Any questions?'

'Am I to return in the plane, or may I stay and take command of the operation, sir?'

'My dear Claude, you already know the answer to that. You are too valuable over here.'

A slightly crestfallen Dupont turned for the door and followed Cartwright out.

Covington's adrenalin rush had subsided and concern had replaced joy.

'Just how safe will this journey be, Commander?'

'As you know, Jack, no plane journey is without risk, but this one has a high degree of safety. Firstly, the Westland Lysander is a very reliable aircraft. It's designed perfectly for the job it has to do. It can land and take off in under fifty yards. It's also painted black from the propeller to the tail fin. You can hear it at night, but you can't see it. Also, at the moment, it's highly unlikely it will be shot down.'

'How can you be sure of that, Commander?'

'Because if you recall, the Germans managed to appropriate a Lysander and have been using it as part of their counter-Auger operation. German AA batteries have been ordered not to fire on any Lysanders, lest there be a German piloting it.'

– CHAPTER THIRTY-SEVEN –

Early afternoon, Thurs, September 7th, 1944, Abwehr HQ, Berlin, Germany.

This does not get any easier, Vilma thought as he sat rigidly in Brietner's office, waiting for him to finish a phone conversation. Just as he'd predicted, Vilma had been called to the general's office a very short time after the latest Auger reports had landed on Brietner's desk. Brietner replaced the receiver and began to shuffle through the papers in front of him.

'This area the map reference refers to, have we had a description?'

'Yes, Herr General. Specifically, it's an area of about one hectare within a larger area of about three hectares. I think it can be best described as an area of scrubby grassland with patches of bog. As far as we can tell, no one lays claim to it and it is left pretty much to the local wildlife. It is surrounded on all sides by mature woodland.'

'Is it under observation?'

'Yes, Herr General. A small group of soldiers are billeted in an old farmhouse three kilometres away. They have set up six-hour watches on rotation to keep eyes on the area from a bivouac in the woods to the south.'

'Are they in wireless contact?'

'Not directly, Herr General, but they do have a communication set up at the farmhouse.'

'Have they reported anything of interest?'

'Not yet, Herr General, but I think tomorrow is the earliest we can expect any activity. They have been briefed to call in anything out of the ordinary.'

Brietner pondered his next statement, then almost without warning pointed an almost accusing forefinger at Vilma.

'Vilma, are you still of the opinion that Operation Auger is an elaborate hoax? Because I must tell you, the High Command agrees with me that the Allies would not have spent so much time and effort moving huge armies of men, embarking them on to ships, and carrying out a major civil engineering project in Kent for no other reason than deception.'

Vilma composed himself before answering.

'May I point out, Herr General, it's common knowledge that the Allies are planning a second invasion. The troop build up commenced weeks ago, long before Auger reared its head. In my professional opinion, there is no hard evidence that Auger is for real.'

Brietner was not satisfied.

'The troop build up may be part of an alternative operation, Vilma. But what about the earthworks near Dover? What about British intelligence employing the services of an expert archaeologist who first mooted the idea that a tunnel under the English Channel may exist? What about the messages we are intercepting from the resistance? There are also Snapdragon and Everest's reports. Sounds like a whole barrow load of evidence to me, Vilma.'

Vilma knew he was participating in an argument he couldn't win, so he decided to change tack.

'I may have some bad news, Herr General. We're almost certain Snapdragon is dead.'

Brietner seemed visibly shocked. He composed himself and his cynicism returned.

'Vilma, I hope this is not a further attempt to impugn the reputation of someone who I, and many others, regard as a hero of the Fatherland.'

Vilma could barely control his anger.

'Herr General, it's my job to bring to your attention anyone who I may have suspicions about, regardless of reputation or how many friends they may have in high places. Especially so when I think I have good grounds for my suspicion.'

Brietner was about to explode and tear a real strip off Vilma, but he managed to restrain himself. He knew Vilma was the best operative the Abwehr had. His brilliance was known, and lauded, well beyond the Abwehr building.

'What makes you think Snapdragon is dead?'

'It began with something Leutnant Muller, our best radio operator, noticed. No two people send Morse code the same way, it's as individual as a fingerprint. In fact, we call it their signature. Muller knows Snapdragon's signature like the back of his hand, and he recently suspected messages that were purportedly from Snapdragon. There were other nuances in the messages that didn't sit right with him as well. Whoever was sending those messages was not Snapdragon. Then, quite by chance, we came upon some information about a body that arrived at a mortuary in London for post-mortem. It had come from Mettlesham, where Snapdragon was based. It was the body of a middle-aged man with the end of the little finger of his left hand missing.'

'I see,' Brietner conceded. 'Do you think the British discovered he was a German agent and disposed of him?'

Vilma shook his head. 'Highly unlikely, Herr General. The British would not conduct a post-mortem on someone they'd eliminated, besides which the body still had pyjamas on, which would suggest natural causes.'

'Are we still in contact with Everest?'

'Yes, Herr General. He has been quite dedicated and it must be quite difficult for him. He holds down a real job, not a fake one like Snapdragon did. He is only "part-time", as it were, and has neither the training nor the skillset a professional operative would have, but he has kept us well informed about the goings on in Kent. By the way, Herr General, we've decided to throw the British a curve ball by ceasing to respond to any messages from this fake Snapdragon. It gives them a problem because they will now be unsure if we have believed anything from Snapdragon to do with Auger.'

'Have they ceased to send these messages?'

'No, Herr General, but they wouldn't stop. To do so would confirm that Snapdragon, one way or another, is no longer in the game. To be honest, Herr General, it doesn't really matter. Whether you think Auger is a hoax or not, there's nothing more to be gleaned in terms of intelligence from Kent. It's this side of the Channel that is now the main focus.'

'That is probably correct, Vilma, but how far are you from gathering the evidence that will disprove Operation Auger is for real?'

Vilma decided now was the time to strike.

'Operatives are, as we speak, interviewing the elder brother of Juste Gilbert. Assuming he can tell us the rough whereabouts of this man-made hillock Covington discovered, we will then need to search for it and determine if indeed it is an entrance to a tunnel. But we will probably be unable to do so by 0900 hours tomorrow, Herr General.'

'You have until 1200 hours, but I will wager before dawn on Saturday a lot more evidence will come to light to prove me right, Vilma.'

– CHAPTER THIRTY-EIGHT –

Early morning, Friday, September 8th, 1944, Cabinet War Rooms, London, England.

In the main committee room, Churchill called the meeting to order. He sat at the head of the table flanked by Eisenhower on one side and Montgomery on the other. Many high-ranking officers occupied the remaining chairs including Group Captain Henshaw, who would oversee the air forces, and Admiral Benson, who would have overall command of naval operations. At a much smaller table, at the opposite end of the room, sat the contingent from the CIU: Bushell and Clegg, Parfitt, Cartwright and Simons, plus Covington and Ledbetter.

'Gentlemen,' Churchill boomed. 'Since we last met I know you have been very busy formulating the plan for the military side of Operation Auger. Well, A-Day is upon the morrow, so with no further ado, I'll ask Field Marshall Montgomery to detail how A-Day will unfold.'

'Thank you, Prime Minister. As you know, gentlemen, whether Auger gets underway or not depends entirely on the Germans deciding to move their forces from Normandy to Calais. It's a journey of about two hundred miles, which we calculate will take them between six and a half and seven hours. At any event, they won't move before sunset as it would leave them vulnerable to air attack. Sunset by the way is at approximately 1945 hours. We don't need to wait for them to arrive at Calais before we get underway, as long as we know they are on their way and fully committed to the move, we can work to our own timetable. We want to simulate a dawn landing at Calais. Sunrise is at 0620 hours, so we calculate the vanguard will need to get underway at around 0315 hours. The vanguard will consist of two heavy cruisers, three light cruisers and twelve destroyers, three of which will be equipped with the new radar. In addition, there will be fifteen cargo vessels manned by navy personnel. They will carry no cargo in order to increase speed and manoeuvrability. Each will be armed with at least six depth charge launchers. They will work in unison with the destroyers armed with the new radar, and as soon as any type 22s are detected, they will saturate the area with depth charges. It's a bit of a scattergun approach, I know, but it should be reasonably effective.'

Admiral Benson raised his hand with a query.

'Do we know where these type 22s are as of this moment?'

Bushell rose to his feet to volunteer the information.

'We know the nine they have at their disposal have left the pens at St Nazaire, presumably when the threat of Auger became a reality to the Germans yesterday. I think it's safe to assume they are lurking somewhere in the Channel.'

Group Captain Henshaw chimed in. 'During daylight hours, coastal command aircraft with anti-submarine capability are quartering the Channel, but we have yet to spot anything.'

Montgomery resumed his position as conductor of the high-ranking orchestra.

'The thing is, gentlemen, we know where they will be early tomorrow morning. The vanguard represents the most clear and present danger, so the type 22s will have to commit to destroying them. The cruisers will open fire at maximum range, but should still be well out of range of the shore batteries. The first of the shells landing on the Calais shoreline will be the signal for the resistance to set off their fireworks display, which is designed to simulate Allied troops, having emerged from the tunnel, beginning to attack the rear of the shore batteries. At the discharge of the first salvos from the cruisers, the main convoy will turn southwest and head for Normandy. We estimate the vanguard will have about thirty minutes firing on the shore batteries before they come within range of their guns. It is then they too will turn southwestward.

'No doubt, gentlemen, it will be an intense battle between the type 22s and the vanguard across the Channel but, God willing, we will at least achieve parity. The main convoy will have at least a thirty-minute head start. By this time, it will be daylight and full air cover will escort the convoy to Normandy. Daylight will also reveal to the Germans that no Allied troops have landed and there was no tunnel. As soon as they realise they have been duped and that a massive invasion force is heading for Calais, the force that made its way from Normandy will have no choice but to head back from whence they came. That's where you come in, Group Captain.'

Henshaw got stiffly to his feet and donned a pair of glasses, even though he had no notes to read. He viewed his audience over the rims of his spectacles.

'The convoy will be at its most vulnerable when it has about-faced and is heading back. We will attack it constantly with continual waves of aircraft. I have two hundred Tempests, Mosquitoes, Mustangs and Lightnings available, collectively armed with rockets, twenty mm cannons, five hundred pound bombs and fifty calibre machine guns. I think they will make their mark.'

Churchill was the next to intervene, addressing General Eisenhower.

'When this vast convoy of men and machinery has relocated to Calais, is it your intention to try and break out from Normandy?'

'No, Prime Minister. There's still a shortage of supplies and reinforcements at the front. But rest assured, as soon as good supply lines have been established, then the advance will begin. It may be even as early as Sunday morning.'

Montgomery continued his oration.

'The convoy heading for Normandy will be of a different make-up than the one on D-Day, with a bias leaning more toward supplies and vehicles, so accordingly there will be more cargo vessels than fighting ships. Remember, this time we don't have to establish a beachhead. Nonetheless, the convoy will land two divisions of infantry. To balance this, at around midday when it is low tide, three divisions of airborne troops will parachute onto the beach. That should keep the transport planes just out of reach of the German howitzers that didn't head for Calais. I think that concludes the itinerary for tomorrow, Prime Minister.'

Churchill carefully placed a half-smoked cigar in the ashtray and surveyed the room before speaking. They were all expecting a pep talk. He started in good humour. He spread his arms wide apart and smiled.

'What could possibly go wrong? Seriously though, gentlemen, I am acutely aware of the courage that will be required by all participants tomorrow. Especially the crews of those ships in the vanguard. It takes a special kind of bravery to go into action when you know there is a good chance you won't be coming back, and yet you go anyway. God willing, casualties will be light. Right, we all know that Operation Auger does not leave port without the Germans obliging us by moving a goodly part of their army. And persuading the Germans of the wisdom of that manoeuvre is the job of Commander Bushell and his merry band of illusionists. Peter, over to you.'

Bushell updated the venerable gathering on all of the CIU's activities. The progress of the deception in Kent, what the resistance had planned, Covington and Ledbetter's ideas, and what the Abwehr had been up to. When he revealed that German forces had already been given the order to make ready to move, Bushell detected the spirit in the room lift appreciably. He also explained the psychological element that was being played out between the hierarchy and the coal face at the Abwehr and how important that was. Bushell concluded his speech and waited for the inevitable questions. Churchill was first.

'From what you say, Peter, there should be a lot of activity in this area just outside Calais tomorrow. If the Germans do swallow this hook, line and sinker and begin to mobilise a sizeable phalanx of their forces in

Normandy, our forces there will see it. That bit is easy. The Germans though will have to issue the order to mobilise some time before they actually move. Do you anticipate securing prior knowledge of this and when do you think that might be?'

Bushell confidently answered the query.

'The first part of the deception, which will be the arrival of some plant at the site of the map reference, will be at 0900 hours. They will be delivered and just left there, as will a couple of trucks about an hour later. These will be parked in nearby woods and camouflaged, but not too well. All to make the Germans think something could be happening. The phoney sappers will make their appearance around 1100 hours. The resistance will continue with their sporadic radio traffic referring to Auger, but will begin to refer to the tunnel entrance in the activity area by a codename, which will basically translate to "Tunnel A". But from midday, a second codename will be introduced, obviously "Tunnel B".

'Later in the afternoon, the last digits of the map reference will make their way onto the airwaves, which coincidently, will mark a spot about ten yards from where the mechanical digger is parked. By the time the Germans decide to do anything about it, it will be too dark to pinpoint the spot accurately or do any exploratory digging. Because we now have a foothold in France, it's far easier to station operatives in occupied territory, and with the help of the resistance, not much gets past our wireless tracking of all German radio traffic. So, yes, Prime Minister, I am very confident we will discover when the German forces are given the order to move.'

Churchill turned to Eisenhower. 'Anything to add, General?'

Eisenhower pointed the butt of his cigarette towards Bushell's table.

'Those guys have almost got me believing there is a goddam tunnel! You gentlemen have all got vast operational experience, so I don't need to stress the importance of timing and intelligence – particularly in this case. We are as ready as we will ever be.'

'Right,' commanded Churchill. 'Peter, numerous ruses are going to be played out during the rest of today and tomorrow, but would you say the most important is the fake sappers being spotted and reported back to German intelligence in Berlin?'

'Well, depending on your degree of optimism, Prime Minister, you could call it the trump card that wins us the pot or the final throw of the dice. But yes, I think your assessment is pretty accurate.'

'So that's what we will go by,' Churchill confirmed. 'As soon as we have confirmation that particular message has winged its way to the Abwehr, we will take it as the first trigger. We will give it the codename "Ace High". When we know that the order has been given for the German forces to move, the codename will be "Full House". When we have final confirmation that the force has mobilised and is actually on the road, that code name will be "Royal Flush". I think that about wraps it up. Good luck, everyone.'

– CHAPTER THIRTY-NINE –

Mid-morning, Friday, September 7th, 1944, Abwehr HQ, Berlin, Germany.

'The French have been busy this morning, Herr Oberst,' Bierhoff said as he entered Vilma's office. 'Two mechanical shovels have turned up at the map reference site. No work was commenced. They just left and the drivers departed in a van. Two trucks, containing we know not what, have been parked in nearby woods. After throwing camouflage nets over them, the drivers also left. There doesn't seem to be any apparent connection between the trucks and the diggers, Herr Oberst. Red herrings, maybe?'

'Any progress with Gilbert's infirm brother?'

'Progress is slow, Herr Oberst, but progress is being made. Though he is very much *compos mentis*, his eyesight is not good. However, he knows what we are looking for and he thinks he knows where to find it. The care home where he lives is right on the coast to the southwest of Calais. We calculate about an hour's drive from where we want to be. Problem is, Herr Oberst, it will be well past General Brietner's deadline of 1200 hours before we can establish anything. They have to first locate the site, which may take some time, drive back and find the nearest army post to transmit whatever they find. I don't expect to hear anything before 1700 hours.'

'Doesn't really matter, Max. What matters is having solid proof before anything moves from Normandy, and that won't be until after dark this evening. Talking of the general. I just had a phone call from him. He's basing himself at High Command HQ until Monday. He's just left. We are to forward all messages to him there and he still wants updates every hour. Anything from Everest?'

'Only what you'd expect, Herr Oberst. Thousands of troops boarding dozens of vessels at ports all along the southeast coast. One thing yesterday afternoon, a few soldiers, about ten, Everest estimates, donned full kit. Helmets with lamps, those gas mask contraptions, the full works, and then they disappeared into the tunnel entrance.'

Vilma considered Bierhoff's last statement, shrugged his shoulders and said, 'The British have to complete the play, Max. Nothing more than show. Otherwise, why make such a song and dance about it, why not wait for dark?'

'How long before the general is contactable, Herr Oberst?'

'About an hour or so.'

'In that case, Herr Oberst, I'll get back to the wireless room. I have a feeling it's going to be a busy day. Should I save everything for the next hour and then bring it to you, Herr Oberst? Then you will be as up-to-date as you can be when you speak to the general.'

'Are all the staff on hand today, Max? As you said,

it's going to be a busy day.'

'Since Auger first reared its head, Herr Oberst, we have operated a shift system in the communications room, so at any one time, we have at least four people on duty. Oberleutnant Schwartz and Leutnant Muller are our senior operatives there, so I've made sure one of them is on duty all the time. Schwartz had duties elsewhere yesterday at HQ High Command, so did a shift swap with Muller. Muller is due to relieve Schwartz at 1800 hours. Schwartz will have done thirty-six hours on duty out of the last forty-eight. I'll be here as cover as well, Herr Oberst.'

'Yes, Max, I don't think either of us will see our own beds for the next forty-eight hours.'

An hour later the phone on Vilma's desk rang. He let it ring again before picking up the receiver.

'Vilma,' he said sharply, knowing full well it was Brietner on the other end.

'Vilma, this is General Brietner. I'm now at HQ and you will be able to contact me directly on this line. High Command are expecting to be kept in touch on a regular basis and I am expecting likewise.'

'Very good, Herr General. Hauptmann Bierhoff is just collating all the latest messages. If I may, could I call you back in ten minutes, Herr General?'

'No later, Vilma,' Bierhoff replied sternly, and put the phone down.

Just as Vilma was about to summon Bierhoff, he walked in clutching a raft of papers.

'Any further developments, Max?'

'Only one item of significance, Herr Oberst, an intercept from the resistance. They've started using two code words about the tunnel entrances. It was slightly confusing until we managed to understand the meaning. One refers to the tunnel on the waste ground and the other to another tunnel entrance. Presumably, the real one and the map reference attached to it is roughly three kilometres north northwest of the waste ground.'

'It's all too overt, Max. With D-Day, we all knew the invasion was coming yes, but none of us had a clue they were going to land in Normandy. It's all too obvious and easy. The British are not that careless unless they want to be. Everything you've given me this morning, Max, it doesn't amount to a hill of beans in terms of the tunnel existing. But Brietner will say the opposite, especially the bit about a handful of soldiers going into a hole in the ground in Kent. Better phone this through, send an abridged version by teleprinter as well would you, Max.'

Vilma picked up the direct line phone to High Command and appraised Brietner of the morning's happenings.

'These fully kitted out men entering the tunnel in Kent is significant, Vilma.'

'With respect, Herr General, it could still be part of the hoax, another convincer.'

'I don't think anything will ever convince you, Vilma, not until the Allies have captured Calais.'

Vilma had neither the spirit nor the inclination to respond.

'Teleprinter copies of these messages have been sent through to you, Herr General,' he said curtly.

– CHAPTER FORTY –

Mid-afternoon, Friday, September 7th, 1944, Abwehr HQ, Berlin, Germany.

The wireless room at the Abwehr was strangely quiet considering what was in the offing. 'Peace been declared?' quipped Bierhoff as he walked in.

He had no sooner finished his sentence than the set Muller was manning sprang to life with the familiar staccato chatter of Morse code. It was a longer-than-normal message, and when it finally ended Muller took it through to the decoding room. He returned five minutes later and, without a word, handed Bierhoff a sheet of note paper. Bierhoff read it, looked at Muller and exclaimed, 'Good God!' and speedily left the room.

He rushed into Vilma's office and silently handed the note to Vilma.

Vilma read it several times, continually shaking his head. He gave the note a lot of deep thought before speaking.

'Well, assuming the British have not devised a way of making twelve sappers appear by magic, I can only think of three explanations of how they got there. They are sappers from the occupying force in Normandy and have been smuggled to the area by the resistance. They were parachuted in overnight, or the first language of our mystery soldiers is French, not English.'

He could see Bierhoff was about to speak.

'And don't even suggest a fourth possibility, Max!'

'I wasn't going to, Herr Oberst. But it does raise the spectre of a third tunnel entrance. Perhaps the British are getting too clever. These sappers appeared out of the woods to the west of the waste ground. The map reference of the second tunnel is to the north-northwest. If they're trying to convince us these soldiers arrived via a tunnel, then where is its entrance?' We know it's not at the waste ground. We'd have seen them pop out of the ground. If they're supposed to have come out of the tunnel entrance where the second map reference is, then they must have gone on one hell of a detour to get to the waste ground. We have no idea where our two operatives are searching with Gilbert's brother, but if they do find the hillock, and there has been no recent disturbance, we've just about proved the whole thing is a hoax. Surely the idea of the tunnel with three entrances would be too preposterous, even for Brietner.

'I wouldn't count on it, Max, but you're right. If we can confirm Covington's hillock isn't a tunnel entrance, then surely they can't mobilise on the possibility there might be a third entrance. Right, Max, contact every operative in Calais and give them the second map reference. Tell them to look out for two of our agents with an elderly civilian. If they're still searching, tell them to help. If they're on the way back, tell them to report to me immediately. Break into the first house they come to with a phone if needs be. Send this lot to Brietner via teleprinter would you, Max?'

'Do you think you will be able to persuade the general of the folly of his ways, Herr Oberst?'

'Let's find out shall we?' said Vilma, lifting the phone.

Brietner sounded almost delirious when Vilma told him of the appearance of the twelve sappers.

'Where did they go after they got to the clearing, Vilma?'

'It's my information, Herr General, that they met some civilians at the site, presumably resistance men. Then they just melted into the woods to the south.'

'Why were they not apprehended?'

'There are only two soldiers on duty at any one time at the bivouac, Herr General. Besides which, they have orders to observe and report only.'

Brietner paused for a minute.

'I think we can now safely assume the idea of a tunnel in the clearing is definitely a hoax, which means the real entrance is where the second map reference is. Stands to reason the British would send a small force to reconnoitre the tunnel first.'

'Doubtful, Herr General. The soldiers came from the west. The new map reference is to the north-northwest.'

'You think it's a double bluff and the actual tunnel entrance is at a third location?'

'No, Herr General, I still think there aren't any entrances or any tunnel either.'

Brietner had come to the end of his tether. 'How do you think those British soldiers got there, Vilma? Do you think they caught the three-fifteen from Paris? I'm going to appraise High Command of this latest information, with the recommendation to mobilise as soon as darkness falls. I will further recommend they station all artillery pieces along the coast to repel a large seaborne force. Also, that two divisions are posted to the west of Calais to repulse an infantry attack from the east, with a further division spread around an area covering four square kilometres of the second map reference.'

'Very good, Herr General,' Bierhoff replied neutrally.

'Any further information comes in, let me know immediately – and, Vilma, I mean immediately.'

– CHAPTER FORTY-ONE –

Mid-afternoon, Friday, September 8th, 1944, Admiralty Buildings, London, England.

Bushell, Covington and Ledbetter sat like expectant fathers in Bushell's office. The Lysander drop-off had been a success and Captain Dupont was reluctantly back in the Admiralty Building. Cartwright joined them, concern showing on his face.

'What's wrong, Cartwright,' Bushell enquired. 'Lost a fiver and found a threepenny bit?'

'Slightly more worrying than losing four pounds, nineteen and ninepence, sir. We might be about to have a giant German spanner thrown in the works. You will recall we had a message yesterday informing us of German agent activity in the Calais area; that they were on the lookout for history academics, teachers, etc. Well, they've apparently struck oil. Juste Gilbert's elder brother is alive, though not too well, and in a nursing home near Calais. Two German officers picked him up at 1000 hours our time. A resistance member questioned the matron of the home, and the same two officers called in yesterday evening, showed the chap some maps and asked him a lot of questions.'

'The Germans would not be taking him for a day trip out of the goodness of their hearts. It means he knows something,' said Bushell anxiously. 'I know they don't have a lot of time to find the hillock or what its significance might be, but it still has the potential to scupper Auger.'

Covington offered some comfort. 'Gilbert never mentioned a brother, so I don't think he could have been involved that often in his expeditions. And as I said, it's really difficult to find. It's not marked on any map. I would have trouble finding it again without a large-scale map of the area.'

'It might actually cause more confusion if they do find the hillock,' Ledbetter added. 'If there is no sign of any entrance in the hillock, from whence did those twelve sappers come? Always assuming the Germans will do as we hope and spot them.'

'True,' Bushell agreed.

'May I add something, Commander?' Covington asked. 'Might it be a good idea if we delay the release of the final two digits relating to the map reference? At least until we know what and if the Germans are going to report on the day's outing with Pascal's brother. It could cause more confusion for them if those numbers are released after they report there is no tunnel at the hillock, and as you say, the sappers had to come from somewhere.'

'Good idea, Jack,' acknowledged Bushell. 'Cartwright, contact our resistance friends and ask them to keep a sharp ear open for any radio traffic between Calais and the Abwehr regarding the possible discovery of a new tunnel entrance. Tell them if they do pick anything up, report it to us without delay. Ask them to delay the radio release of those last digits until we say so as well.'

*

Once Cartwright had departed, the trio spent the next hour, like many millions did during precious downtime, discussing what they were going to do after the war.

'Whatever I end up doing,' Ledbetter said with a grin, 'it will seem very boring compared to the last three weeks!'

The reverie was rudely interrupted by the sound of someone running down the corridor. Cartwright galloped into the room.

'Sir, it's Ace High!'

– CHAPTER FORTY-TWO –

*Late afternoon, Friday, September 8th, 1944, Admiralty
Building, London, England.*

Bushell, Covington and Ledbetter were again playing the waiting game.

'God, I now know what Barnes Wallace felt like sitting at that airfield waiting for news of the Dambusters raid,' observed Ledbetter.

'It's something you never get used to, Frank,' Bushell agreed.

'Just as a matter of pessimistic interest, Commander. If Auger was to unravel, have you thought what your next move would be?' Covington asked.

'At the end of the day, Jack, I'm basically in the employ of His Majesty's Government, a humble functionary – if a well-paid one. In other words, I do my master's bidding. If this goes wrong, I'm not sure if I'll ever be asked to contribute again. In this game, you're only as good as your last assignment. But I never countenance failure, Jack. It clouds your judgement.'

More speedy footsteps in the corridor heralded the arrival of a very excited Cartwright.

'It's Full House, sir,' he blurted.

'Excellent! So far, so good. Inform Number Ten immediately would you, Cartwright, and I think we now have a direct line to Camp Griffiss, so make sure General Eisenhower is brought up to speed as well.'

'Well, Commander, another bridge crossed,' Ledbetter said with as smile.

'Yes, but we still have yet to hear about Monsieur Gilbert's day out,' cautioned Covington.

'Good point, Jack,' Bushell conceded, 'but with the possibility of a third entrance now in the mix, it may not matter what they find.'

A very crestfallen Cartwright re-entered the office.

'I'm sorry to report, sir, that our resistance colleagues have just been in contact and admitted to an almighty cock up. When they first broadcast about the second tunnel entrance, they just added a couple of numbers to the Eastings and Northings. In other words, an area about two miles away. The trouble is, no one bothered to consult a map. The area in question is a three-acre lake.'

The good cheer left the office faster than the air from a burst balloon.

After a few seconds head shaking, Bushell spoke.

'Cartwright, contact the resistance immediately and tell them under no circumstances to correct the map reference numbers. The Germans will then strongly suspect something's gone wrong from our side. We can hope the Germans have not done their homework and they are in blissful ignorance about tunnel entrance number two being underwater. And we do still have the mythical third entrance. At any event, it's out of our hands now.'

– CHAPTER FORTY-THREE –

Late afternoon, Friday, September 7th, 1944, Abwehr HQ,
Berlin, Germany.

Vilma had a feeling of complete resignation as he slumped back in his chair for the umpteenth time. *It's over*, he thought. He raised his head to greet Bierhoff as he entered the office.

'Ask not for whom the bell tolls, Max.'

'I wouldn't start pulling on the rope just yet, Herr Oberst. We've been studying maps to try and locate where the third mythical entrance these British soldiers were supposed to have emerged from, using our best efforts to try and figure out where Covington's hillock might be. Just as a cross reference, we checked where the second map reference was. Somebody, somewhere has dropped an almighty clanger, Herr Oberst. It's a lake.'

'Well, that's two entrances blown out of the water, Max. And I've been giving some thought to all these mind games and all these tunnels. We now know entrances A and B are hoaxes. Entrance A is the one the British have gone out of their way to convince us is a hoax – the hoax hoax if you like. Entrance B is the one they wanted us to think is real, just long enough to divert us from looking for the entrance that the soldiers really came out of. Which is Covington's hillock. It may not be too late, Max, if we can get word from Calais on what Gilbert's search found.'

'We have operatives combing the area in and around Calais trying to track them down, Herr Oberst.'

The pair spent the next hour in very much the same vein as their counterparts were doing at the Admiralty Building in London – sitting around waiting. Vilma swivelled in his chair to look out of the window. Ribbons of pink spoke of a spectacular sunset as the sun, slowly transitioning from dark pink to a fiery magenta, sank towards the western horizon.

'They'll soon be on their way, Max,' said Vilma, a note of hopelessness in his voice. Before Bierhoff could answer, a head appeared around the door.

'Beg pardon, Herr Oberst, Herr Hauptmann. There's a priority one message coming in from the farmhouse billet near the first map reference area.'

'Go and see what it is, Max.'

Five minutes later, Bierhoff returned accompanied by Oberleutnant Schwartz.

Bierhoff proffered the sheet of paper. Vilma waived it away.

'Read it to me, Max. My eyes ache.'

Bierhoff tried to speak in a calm, collected manner.

'It's from an Oberleutnant Fischer, Herr Oberst – he was one of the two operatives who took Gilbert out. Gilbert is absolutely adamant he found the exact place, but there was no hillock. What was there was a new army storage facility and repair shop. It has just been completed.'

Vilma gave Schwartz a stony stare.

'Just how sure is Gilbert of his bearings, Schwartz?'

'According to Fischer, Herr Oberst, one hundred per cent. Fischer also said that the surrounding area seemed to correspond with the aerial photographs taken in forty-three.'

'That means we now have irrefutable proof that all the supposed tunnel entrances do not exist. This time Brietner will have to listen.'

Vilma picked up the phone, pulled it away from his ear and looked quizzically at it.

'This phone is not working. Are all the phone lines down?'

'Don't think so, Herr Oberst,' Schwartz replied. 'Fischer got through by telephone. I'll go and check.'

'Max, if we can't get through to Brietner, a courier is going to have to take this information to him at High Command.'

'But that would take an hour, Herr Oberst. The convoy will probably be underway by then,' Bierhoff protested.

'What other choice do we have? They shouldn't have got too far and they have yet to start. Sunset is a bit later in Normandy than here in Berlin.'

'All lines between here and High Command HQ are down, Herr Oberst. Doesn't seem to be any obvious reason,' Schwartz reported as he returned.

'Does that mean the teleprinter is also out?'

'I'm afraid so, Herr Oberst,' Schwartz confirmed.

'Right, Max, find me a courier and a fast vehicle.'

'Beg pardon, Herr Oberst,' Schwartz interrupted, 'but there might be another way.'

'We are all ears, Uwe.'

'If you give me a few minutes in the communications room, Herr Oberst, I'm sure I could contact General von Runstedt's HQ at Normandy, but it would be by signal, not telephone. It would have to bypass General Brietner, of course.'

'That may be no bad thing, Uwe. Send this message to von Runstedt's HQ. Mark it as priority one, and start and end it with the Abwehr verification code, so there's no doubt who it's from. Send: 'All tunnel entrances now confirmed non-existent. Therefore, tunnel must be a hoax.'

'Very good, Herr Oberst, I'll get on it right away,' said Schwartz, turning on his heel.

'Might it have been prudent to recommend calling off the mobilisation, Herr Oberst?' asked Brietner.

'I don't have that authority, Max. Neither does von Runstedt. He'd have to run it by High Command first, and he's in constant contact with them. He may well put it all on hold though, until he gets the yay or nay.'

'Should I put a courier on standby, Herr Oberst, in case Schwartz can't get through?'

Vilma shook his head. 'If Schwartz can't get in contact, it's probably best that I go and see Brietner myself. He's liable just to ignore any written notes, but if I'm there I can give full details of everything that's happened over the last few hours. A piece of paper can't do that.'

The two of them impatiently awaited Schwartz's return. The ten-minute wait seemed like half an hour.

'I got through, Herr Oberst,' beamed the returning Schwarz, 'wasn't as difficult as I anticipated. Herr Oberst, I hope I did right but I have asked the radio operator I was in contact with to inform us of the outcome.'

'You most certainly did do right, Uwe. Well done. Inform us as soon as you receive word would you?'

Vilma and Bierhoff exhaled simultaneously which brought a smile to both their faces.

'Have we called this right, Max?' said Vilma with a note of doubt in his voice.

'In many ways, we were fighting on two fronts, Herr Oberst. A combination of British deviousness and French playacting on one side, and one of our own generals, who seems to have lost his grip on reality, regardless of how much common sense is placed in front of him. I think an honourable draw is the most we can hope for.'

The pair spent the next half hour conducting a post-mortem on the whole operation and concluded they had been thorough and that no other conclusion could have been arrived at.

Schwartz marched in, this time with an even bigger grin on his face.

'The taskforce that was going to head for Calais has been stood down, Herr Oberst. You two have single-handedly saved Germany.'

'A bit of an exaggeration,' said Vilma ruefully, 'besides which, I don't think I want the responsibility.'

'General Brietner will be looking for a target for his anger after such a slap down,' warned Bierhoff.

'I'm expecting a call any minute,' said Vilma, nodding at the phone.

'I doubt it, Herr Oberst,' said Schwartz, 'the phone's not working.'

A tired but relieved smile broke out on Vilma's face.

'Uwe, you've earned your salary this month,' Vilma complemented, 'you've hardly been off duty the last few days.'

'Leutnant Muller relieves me at 2000 hours, Herr Oberst. I'll get some rest.'

'Shoot off now, Uwe, we'll cover for you till Muller gets in. After the lord mayor's show, it should be a much quieter night.'

'Thank you. Goodnight, Herr Oberst, goodnight, Herr Hauptmann.' He clicked his heels smartly and made for the door.

'In our store room, Max, do we have any army cots, blankets and what have you?'

'I'm sure we have, Herr Oberst, should I send for some?'

'Please. I'd better be on hand. There is sure to be an enquiry into all this and it may just start as soon as the telephone lines are fixed. Once Muller gets in, you might as well head for home as well, Max.'

'If it's all the same to you, Herr Oberst, I'll help myself to one of those cots and bed down in my office. If the phones are down, you won't be able to reach me at home.'

– CHAPTER FORTY-FOUR –

2am, Saturday, September 9th, 1944, Abwehr HQ, Berlin, Germany.

Vilma was in a deep sleep when Bierhoff walked in, still buttoning up his tunic.

'Herr Oberst, sorry to wake you, but Muller has just picked up a message from Everest. We had earlier picked up messages from the resistance, as expected, giving out the final numbers of the map references. Of course, these are now irrelevant, so you weren't disturbed. However, Muller's message is slightly more concerning. His dedication to duty is to be applauded, Herr Oberst. As A-Day was approaching, he waited to keep the field in Kent under observation. The Allies must now know that we have not mobilised the force from Normandy, so one would expect the troops billeted in the Kent field either to bed down for the night, or perhaps return to barracks. Those troops did mobilise, Herr Oberst, but did not return to barracks. They marched down to Dover harbour and embarked onto troop carriers.'

Vilma was not yet fully conscious, so his brain was

having trouble processing what Bierhoff had told him. He gathered himself before speaking.

'There could be any number of reasons why they would do that, Max, but we need to find out the actual reason and quickly.'

A confused-looking Muller was framed in the doorway.

'Herr Oberst, a message from the farmhouse where the soldiers watching the clearing are billeted. It simply says they have been relieved by troops from the Normandy force.'

Vilma grabbed the nearest phone, put the receiver to his ear and then immediately replaced it.

'Phones are still out. What the hell is going on? Muller, contact that farmhouse again and ask them to clarify their last message. Ask them to give us a report of what is going on around them.'

'Right away, Herr Oberst.'

'Max, do you think they've changed their minds? Did Brietner get wind of our message to von Runtstedt and persuade High Command that he is right and we are wrong?'

'If Brietner had got wind of the message, Herr Oberst, he would have turned up here to confront us.'

The two came up with a list of possible reasons that would explain the apparent chaos. None of which were satisfactory. Muller once again stood in the doorway, his confused expression replaced by one of dread.

'Herr Oberst, the farmhouse reports the arrival in the area of hundreds of troops. A large convoy of vehicles, armour and men began to arrive on the western outskirts of Calais around midnight.'

'How could this have happened?' asked Vilma,

almost pleadingly. 'The message Schwartz sent was clear. It was acknowledged and acted upon.'

At the German-Swiss border, a smartly dressed man in his early thirties disembarked from a train on the German side. He had an air of calm authority, with no hint of arrogance. He waited patiently in the queue to be processed at the border gate. When it was his turn, he handed the German officer his identity card. The guard examined it by the light of a torch and read aloud the information.

'Jean Schwab, from Berne, occupation civil servant, seconded to the Red Cross for the duration.'

The guard checked that the photo matched the face, and satisfied that it did, he waived the man through.

'Thank you, Herr Schwab.'

The man repeated the process at the Swiss gate, made the short walk to the station and boarded the train bound for Berne. He waited until the train was about ten minutes into its journey before heading to the toilet. He locked the door behind him, took out his wallet and extracted his identity card. But it wasn't the one he'd just used at the two border gates. He took one last look at it, methodically tore it into small pieces, and flushed it down the bowl. It bore the name Oberleutnant Uwe Schwartz.

– CHAPTER FORTY-FIVE –

4am, Saturday, September 9th, 1944, Abwehr HQ, Berlin, Germany.

Vilma's emotions were a worrying cocktail of anger, frustration, confusion and tiredness. Despite his state of mind, he endeavoured to stay in control and unravel the enigma that had been the last few hours. The first piece of the jigsaw arrived in the form of Leutnant Muller. He spoke in hoarse, shocked tones.

'Herr Oberst, the engineer has now fixed the issue with the phones. The main cable connecting our system with the outside network had been disconnected. We've also had reports from our radar stations on the Channel coast. They are picking up a rash of very strong signals from all along the southeast coast of England, which basically means that multiple large vessels are leaving port.'

A dreadful silence filled the office. All three were beginning to think the unthinkable. Very deliberately and with a huge sense of foreboding, Vilma lifted the phone.

'Get me High Command'

While he was waiting, he addressed Muller.

'Get hold of von Runstedt's HQ if you can. We don't know if he's still in Normandy or travelled with the convoy. Try and get their version of events.'

A voice on the telephone told Vilma he was through to High Command.

'This is Oberst Vilma. One of our operatives, an Oberleutnant Uwe Schwartz was carrying out duties with you on Thursday. I want to know who he was working for and with. Call me back.'

Vilma stared at the ceiling with his hands behind his head while Bierhoff paced backward and forward across the room, an awful realisation beginning to dawn on them. Head and shoulders slumped forward, Muller returned. The phone rang before he could speak. He picked up the receiver after the third ring.

'Vilma,' he croaked. Vilma didn't utter a word until he ended the conversation with 'thank you' and slowly put the phone down. He raised his eyes to Bierhoff.

'No one from here called Schwartz was at the HC building on Thursday, nor was an operative requested. Muller, talk me through the conversation you had with Schwartz about the shift swap.'

'I think it was Wednesday, Herr Oberst. He said HC wanted a ranking wireless operator with top security clearance for a few hours on Thursday. That meant it had to be him or me. He volunteered and suggested we swapped shifts.'

'Did Schwartz run this by you, Max?'

Bierhoff nodded his confirmation.

'High Command do borrow our operatives from time to time, Herr Oberst, and as he and Muller here had sorted out cover. There didn't seem to be an issue, so I okayed it.'

In Vilma's mind, the dread was becoming a reality.

'Schwartz wanted to make sure he was in charge of the communications room at the vital time.'

'I've just begun to put a few two and twos together, Herr Oberst.' Bierhoff admitted. 'In the days before we went on our trip to the Paris museum, Schwartz was talking about Roman history and how we all could learn from it. He was letting me know subliminally that he was the one that should accompany me on that operation to ensure we did get the map and photographs. Oh God, something else has just dawned on me, Herr Oberst. Schwartz didn't take a punt in duping Pascal into describing Covington – he already knew he was tall with a shock of unruly hair!'

'And there's another thing,' Vilma added. 'Schwartz spent some time in England on student exchange when he was in university just before the war. That's one of the reasons we recruited him.'

'Are we in big trouble, Herr Oberst?' Muller asked nervously.

'Possibly,' Vilma answered. 'But I fancy nowhere near as much as General Brietner is going to be.'

– CHAPTER FORTY-SIX –

At exactly 5am on A-Day, HMS *Warspite* discharged her fifteen-inch guns at the shore batteries on the coast of Calais to signal the start of Operation Auger. The barrage continued for thirty minutes and then ceased as the vanguard turned to the southwest, a manoeuvre that left a lot of confused Germans. To the west, Germans peered into the half-light, trying to spot Allied troops who had surfaced after a long trek under the Channel. Troops who were destined never to make an appearance.

The day, as expected, was one of bloody attrition. The vanguard's attack on Calais did its job, but at a high cost. As expected, the type 22s caused havoc, with them and the shore batteries inflicting heavy damage. One of the light cruisers was sunk and another was badly damaged. Both heavy cruisers sustained some damage. Four destroyers were lost and several damaged, but thankfully, none of the three carrying the new radar. Of the fifteen cargo ships fitted with the depth charge launchers, six were sunk and three were badly damaged.

But despite the heavy casualties, the ploy worked. The depth charge spewing cargo ships completely fooled the submarines, sinking two of them and badly damaging a third. The three radar-guided destroyers accounted for another type 22 and put another out of action. When it dawned on them what was happening, the remaining type 22s chased after the main convoy with the destroyers hot in pursuit. Again the state-of-the-art radar system proved successful, with two more of the subs being put out of action.

With the full realisation of the massive error they had made and of the real destination of the armada, the Germans had no option but to send the convoy of men and armour back to Normandy. The fifteen-mile train made a dandy target for the ground attack aircraft. Tempests, Mosquitoes, Mustangs and Lightnings poured out of the sky in unrelenting waves, battering the convoy back to Normandy. Only ten per cent of the artillery pieces made it back and almost none of the support trucks. Nearly half of the tanks were lost.

At low tide, three divisions of airborne troops landed almost unmolested on the Normandy beaches. By 1400 hours, the area was like a small city at rush hour. Landing craft of different sizes deposited all manner of vehicles and men on the beaches, while larger vessels did likewise at the Mulberry harbours. Much-needed ammunition, reinforcements, artillery, tanks, rations and, above all, fuel started heading for the front.

At dawn on Sunday morning, the Allies launched their attack. The fighting was bitter and costly, but superior numbers began to make a difference and by late morning cracks began to appear along the line. By midday, the advance became unstoppable and the Allies gained five miles on A-Day Plus One.

With the type 22s no longer a credible threat and the

234

Luftwaffe making only the occasional appearance, daily convoys were landing at Normandy in virtual safety. Supply lines were regularly maintained, enabling the Allies to make steady progress into France.

Operation Auger had more than achieved its aim.

Later on Saturday, General Brietner was arrested, stripped of all rank and was never seen again. Vilma, Bierhoff and Muller were found to be not at fault at the subsequent investigation, which concluded that, despite Schwartz's treachery, the debacle of A-Day could have been prevented had the trio been listened to rather than Brietner. In fact, Vilma was made head of the Abwehr and promoted to general. Bierhoff followed Vilma up the ladder and was made an Oberst.

When the war was in its final throes, Bushell, Vilma's old adversary, recommended that both Vilma and Bierhoff be searched for and offered employment by the Allies to keep tabs on the new enemy – the Soviet Union. Posts which they both took up.

– CHAPTER FORTY-SEVEN –

Monday morning, September 11th, 1944, London, England.

Bushell walked out of Downing Street and headed for the Admiralty Building, the congratulations of the prime minister still ringing in his ears. Churchill had been fulsome in his praise and passed on further commendations from both Eisenhower and Montgomery. Bushell had winced slightly when Churchill was waffling on about how the success of Operation Auger had all but won the war for the Allies, and other statements that Bushell thought were slight exaggerations. The truth was that Bushell loved his work. He never lost sight of the fact that this was war and people died, but his positive mindset of 'If I succeed in this, how many lives will it save?' easily overrode the casualty rate. But the real enjoyment came from the mental cut and thrust, trying to outwit an enemy whose ability you had the utmost respect for.

Churchill also intimated that formal recognition was coming his way. He was going to receive a knighthood. Bushell told Churchill he was both delighted and humbled to receive the accolade, but quickly pointed out the contribution of his team, especially that of Covington and Ledbetter. Churchill assured him they would not be overlooked.

As expected, Covington and Ledbetter were waiting for him. They were both thrilled with the news of Bushell's impending knighthood and their congratulations were both warm and sincere. They were halfway down their second cup of tea when Bushell casually let it drop that they both had an OBE coming their way, as indeed had Clegg. Ledbetter could not contain his delight. He leapt up, ran to the door and bawled 'Cartwright!' down the corridor. As Cartwright trotted down the corridor to meet him, Ledbetter pulled his wallet from his pocket and yanked out a ten-shilling note. He handed it to Cartwright with the instruction to find the first open place and buy a bottle of champagne.

The group spent a pleasant couple of hours holding an informal post-mortem on Operation Auger.

'I have to say,' Ledbetter admitted. 'I've never had a feeling of relief in my life like I had when Cartwright came in and announced Royal Flush, especially after we'd found out the Germans, with a little help, had found the hillock.'

'Yes, it was touch and go for a while,' Bushell admitted, 'but, Jack, it must be a bit disappointing, knowing your study site is now under a large building.'

'I have been thinking about that, Commander. I was fairly certain Monsieur Gilbert senior would not be able to find it. As I said, it is very isolated and overgrown, probably even more so now. But what struck me was, what a strange place for the Germans to build such a thing. It's at least two miles from a main road and building an access road to it would not be easy. I could understand it if it was some sort of secret establishment, but a depot that would be in constant use – it just doesn't make sense.'

Covington was not a happy man.

'Commander,' he asked. 'Do we know exactly where this building is supposed to be?'

'We intercepted the message from the agents who found it. I'm assuming they gave a grid reference. Let's go to the map room and pick up Cartwright on the way.'

Cartwright studiously examined the large-scale map of north-western France that Bushell had pinned to the wall. Having checked the numbers, he indicated a spot on the map with the point of a pencil.

'That's it, Mr Covington, give or take fifty yards in any direction.'

Covington replaced Cartwright's pencil with his forefinger and studied the area around the end of his digit.

'Well, Commander,' he concluded. 'I may not know exactly where the hillock is, but it sure as hell isn't there.'

'You sure, Jack?' Bushell questioned.

'One hundred per cent.'

'Well, well, well,' Bushell chortled, 'looks as if not only did Monsieur Gilbert get taken for a ride by the Germans – he took them for one as well! Good for him!'

The trio continued their not-too-serious dissection of Auger.

'If you look at the timetable of events,' Covington reflected, 'that is, the time gap between the German's discovery of the hillock and Full House being ratified. There must have been some crossed wires or their communications were not up to snuff. I mean they would have had time to assess the latest intel, decided no entrances, no tunnel and cancelled the whole thing.'

'Perhaps they did and the message failed to get through,' said Bushell, his voice loaded with suggestion.

Covington and Ledbetter stared open-mouthed at one another, and then at Bushell.

'Come on, Commander,' urged Ledbetter, 'spill the beans!'

'I'm sure you understand there are certain things I can't reveal, but I can tell you that I had a small insurance policy, which circumstances dictated that I had to cash in. But make no mistake, gentlemen, it does not detract one iota from your contribution to Auger. I can assure you we could not have done it without you.'

'Any other titbits?' Covington encouraged.

'Well,' Bushell relented, 'I guess letting you in on some of the wrinkles won't do any harm. You may recall we were a bit concerned when we found out the Germans had discovered that you two had stand-ins in the Kent field. It was always my intention to make sure they found out about that. You see, I always meant to run the hoax hoax and the real hoax side by side, and having four of you instead of two of you would add to their confusion. It would also encourage them to follow up with the museum lead. It was top secret, this one – even Major Clegg didn't know about it.'

'Well, I'm glad the four of us were of use!' Ledbetter grinned, 'You mean you left a Lysander lying around in France for the Germans to find, just to photograph Burdock and Tinwald?'

'Ah! Confession time,' Bushell admitted. 'That really did happen – but what a marvellous stroke of luck! The photos the Lysander took were far more convincing than the ones I was going to get Snapdragon to take.'

A smiling Cartwright entered and handed a note to Bushell. Bushell read it and grinned.

'It's from Babs. She sends her warmest congratulations. Says you can have the rest of the week off and wants you both back in work by Monday.'

All three smiled, now knowing that Operation Auger was over. All the staff involved were called into Bushell's office and final fond farewells were said. The pair moved toward the door and half-turned to say one last goodbye and Bushell donned his glasses to study some papers on his desk. Without raising his head, he said, 'By the way, gentlemen, when you leave your hotel, you will take your Roman trinkets with you, won't you?'

Covington and Ledbetter looked at each other, shook their heads one final time and headed off down the corridor.

– CHAPTER FORTY-EIGHT –

Autumn, 1961, just outside Calais, France.

C ovington and Ledbetter had, at long last, managed to fulfil their wartime pledge to each other. To return to France and explore thoroughly the small, horseshoe-shaped hill that Juste Gilbert had shown Covington back in 1939. Both were now Cambridge professors and their work left them with precious little free time to indulge themselves on what they both agreed, would be the wildest of goose chases. In the intervening years, they had both, from time to time, tried to find any sliver of evidence that the Romans had even begun, let alone completed, the herculean task of excavating a tunnel under the English Channel. The search had been fruitless. But like an itch you can't scratch, they both felt the need to erase, once and for all, the minute percentage of possibility that the tunnel had, at very least, been started upon. Excavating the small hill would finally enable them to scratch that itch.

Ledbetter was piloting the mechanical digger they'd hired, and using the back bucket, he carefully scraped away a few inches of topsoil and then withdrew.

Covington clambered up the slope with a small rake and looked for any sort of clue. When he was satisfied there was nothing of interest, he waved Ledbetter back in again.

After they'd repeated the exercise several times, Covington noticed the soil was getting increasingly shaley. He signalled Ledbetter to stop and once more scrambled up the slope, virtually on all fours. He carefully raked away where the bucket had last passed and, without warning, a fist-sized hole suddenly appeared. Clawing with his bare hands, Covington managed to widen the hole enough to peer through and having done so, reached for his torch. He directed the beam through the aperture and froze.

Ledbetter sensed something was amiss and turned the key to cut the engine.

'Everything, OK, Jack?' he enquired.

Covington regained his composure and slowly turned to Ledbetter.

'Frank,' he uttered hoarsely. 'I think you'd better come and see this.'